SISTERS

A Promise Kept

Bradley L. Candie

Inspired by the lives of:
Gertrude Cox
Shirley Weldon
Sarah Walker

ISBN: 979-8-9859848-0-4 *(Paperback)*
ISBN: 979-8-9859848-1-1 *(E-Book)*
Library of Congress Control Number: 2022906068

First Paperback Edition 2022

Cover Design by *@TheiDentityCorp*
Author Photo by *iDentityPics.com*
Cover Photos:
Front Top from Left to Right: *Gertrude Cox & Shirley Weldon*
Front Bottom: *Sarah Walker*
Back Bottom: *Helen Smith*

Printed in the United States of America

Published by The iDentity Corporation
113-B Midland Ave., Kearny, NJ 07032
www.TheiDentityCorporation.com
(833) 4iDentity

SISTERS: *A Promise Kept*

Bradley L. Candie

Dedication

This book is dedicated to the memory of:

Gertrude Cox, Mother
Shirley Weldon, Aunt
Sarah Walker, Aunt

And to each family member who fought and
continues to fight the battle against cancer.

May your memory live on forever.

CONTENTS

Preface

I am tired. The process of writing Sisters: *A Promise Kept* has honestly been exhausting and emotionally draining. I have had to sit with and process through all my unresolved, painful issues, thoughts, and feelings that have resurfaced during this journey. I do not know why I was chosen to give birth to this work, but I humbly submit to the God of my understanding and accept His will to see this mission to fruition.

Sisters: *A Promise Kept* is inspired by the lives of three incredibly strong and courageous women: my mother, Gertrude Cox and Aunts, Shirley Weldon and Sarah Walker. This work depicts the lives of three sisters and their shared experiences, battles, and triumphs in the face of being diagnosed with breast cancer.

Throughout my life, I have watched cancer unapologetically take the lives of many loved ones. If you are not familiar with or have not experienced the destructive path of cancer, consider yourself blessed. Cancer not only affects those infected with the dreaded disease, it affects those who are the caretakers. It leaves them unforgettable images, sounds, and emotions that can haunt the deep, dark recesses of the mind.

As I have often heard throughout my life, to whom much is given, much is required. I have been repeatedly blessed by such a dedicated, invested, and nurturing family. It is my obligation to create works to honor a family that has sacrificed for my betterment. Sisters: *A Promise Kept* will forever immortalize the names and memories of those family members who are no longer with us and pay tribute to those who continue their fight.

It is my duty to speak on behalf of those who have lost their voice. It is my responsibility to stand in the gap and remain encouraged for the tired, weary, and worn. It is my honor to carry the torch for the survivors. I refuse to surrender to the will of cancer. I will fight cancer with every fiber of my being, with every breath in my body, and with my last ounce of strength.

I charge you with the awesome responsibility of celebrating life. Cancer's mission is to silence the disheartened. Do not allow cancer to steal your voice. Scream, yell, shout, dance, cry, laugh, and rejoice. Let cancer hear you. Let cancer know you are not afraid. Let it be your absolute resolute to take your power back and to no longer be a voluntary victim. Fight! Fight! Fight! I can hear you. It sounds so beautiful.

Acknowledgements

I would like to first and foremost thank my Lord and Savior Jesus Christ for entrusting me with this vision and equipping me with the necessary tools to complete the mission.

*"I can do all things through Christ
which strengtheneth me."*

(Philippians 4:13, KJV)

I would like to express my sincere gratitude to each and every friend and cast member who lent their talents to bringing Sisters, the play, to fruition. We started this journey back in 2008 with a simple table reading in the living room of my two bedroom apartment not knowing where this path would take us, but believing that there was a purpose in this creation. We cried and consoled each other as we exposed our personal experiences and vulnerability as we watched our loved ones and own selves fight the battle against cancer. Our faith and shear belief in the power of prayer birthed several opportunities to take Sisters from my living room to the pulpits of Big Bethel AME Church and Tabernacle Baptist Church in Atlanta, Georgia. We heard the applause and experienced the magnitude of the impact that Sisters had on a live audience. From the pulpit to the stage, we made our first theatre debut at TP Productions Dinner Theatre in East Point, Georgia in 2018 playing to a sold out house each night. If you had never believed in Sisters, the play, there would have never been Sisters: *A Promise Kept.*

I would like to thank my first cousins, George Weldon and Wendy Walker for allowing me to share their mother's lives and experiences with the world. Thank you for braving this journey with me to ensure that our mother's memories would live on.

I would like to thank each and every family member who shared their stories of battling cancer with me, as well as their experiences caretaking for those on the battlefield fighting for their lives. Your strength, courage and determination to fight the good fight provided the necessary inspiration and motivation to complete this mission.

I wish to thank my best friend, Gregory Caldwell for his unwavering dedication to our friendship and brotherhood. You have motivated me when I felt like I could not go on. You have inspired me when I felt defeated. You have loved me through the darkest times of my life. You are my teacher, my mentor, my brother, and will always be my best friend. I truly love you Greg and thank you from the bottom of my heart for your presence in my life. Brothers in Song Sing on.

Lastly, I would like to thank the wounded child in me for not succumbing to depression, low self-esteem, suicidal thinking, and fear. Your process has not been easy. Many did not understand, but you trusted that God would make a way to bring you out of days riddled with anxiety, depression and self-hatred. Your faith wavered many days, but you stood the course of time. Thank you for giving US a chance to not only exist, but to LIVE. You are enough!

Introduction

Cancer's purpose is to steal your voice and to silent the disheartened mentally, physically, emotionally and spiritually. Within the pages of this book is an honest inspired story of three women who found the strength to reclaim their voice; and in doing so, their freedom- the freedom to cry, yell, scream, laugh, smile and ultimately, to live. If you are currently living with this reality it will be your responsibility to free yourself from the fear and uncertainty that cancer attempts to instill in you and to not willingly accept the outcome planned for you. You have the power to control your life's path, your decisions, and your healing.

No, I have not been diagnosed with cancer. No, I do not know what it feels like to personally hear the words, "you have cancer" and to experience the gambit of emotions that may flood the soul. I submit that as a caretaker for family members who have been diagnosed with cancer, I truly have been profoundly affected mentally, physically, emotionally, and spiritually by this disease. I have spent the majority of my life watching how cancer slowly destroys the dignity of a person. I have experienced feeling angry, helpless and hopeless. I have had to come to my own resolve and level of acceptance. Cancer is not a figment of my imagination. Cancer is alive and real to me. It has a face, a name, and a presence. It has infected my memories and has offered no apology. Though the scars may not be visible to the naked eye, I am scarred. However, I am healing.

By reading this book, some will be able to cry and even rejoice for the first time. Some will come to the conclusion that they are not alone in this healing process. Others will use the dialogue of certain characters found within the book to find their voice and to communicate their experiences for them. This book will give you permission to reconnect with perhaps some painful memories and to write a different ending. You will have the opportunity to experience whatever it is that you wish to experience while being in a safe space; however, this will only transpire if you give yourself permission. Your resolve is in your hands.

Sisters: *A Promise Kept* will take you on a journey of self-awareness, healing, and empowerment. It will remind you that no matter what your circumstances may be, cancer does not and will not have the final say so in your life. You are not a voluntary victim without a voice. You are powerful! You are victorious!

Do not allow fear to stop you from going on this journey. Some will ask why would they want to relive such a traumatic situation over again? All anyone would want to do is to move on and not remember. I offer this explanation: if you define a situation as being traumatic, it will be traumatic. If you define a situation as an opportunity to heal, it will be and do just that. I truly believe that this book has the power to heal and to uplift. Read Sisters: *A Promise Kept* and become equipped with the necessary tools to live the best life you can ever live. Take the challenge. Confront your fears. Deal with your thoughts so that we can end the tumultuous reign of cancer forever.

CHAPTER ONE

Momma

I don't remember much about the night that Momma died. I try to block it out as much as possible, but sometimes, when I'm not thinking, a memory or two comes rushing back to me. Sometimes, the memories are so overwhelming that it knocks me clear off my feet.

I do remember that night had fallen. It was pitch black outside, as the old-folks used to say. I remember the faint sound of the window pane rattling back and forth...'cause it was storming outside. The wind was blowing something terrible, as the rain beat down on the house.

Back during that time, the old people would make everyone sit together in one room until the storm had passed. You couldn't talk or barely move. Momma made us turn off the TV...pull every socket out the wall...and begin to pray. You better not talk during the storm. God help you if you did. Momma would look at you some kind of way - a way that could stop you dead in your tracks.

As the thunder pounded, the old house shook with such force. It just seemed like...all it would take would be one good-old *crack* and the house would come a-crashing down. They sure don't build houses like this anymore! It stood up against the worst storms I had ever seen. The lightning lit up the house and scared us half to death. God was talking and we sure were listening. Some of my older aunts and uncles would tell stories of when it stormed, like it did the night Momma died - "it was God's way of bringing the old home to Heaven and birthing the new into the world." Momma never stirred a bit during the storm. She just laid there with her eyes fixed on the ceiling, or at least it seemed. To me, she was staring God right in the eyes.

There was nothing peaceful about her death...nothing peaceful at all. Her breathing was off, some kind of way. It was forceful and labored. I swear I could hear each and every breath that she took. Each time she exhaled, I prayed to God that it wouldn't be her last.

As I stood on the side of her bed, every once in a while I would lock eyes with my younger sister Sarah. We didn't say anything to each other, but just looked. You know that kind of look that could send a chill right down the center of your spine? It was that kind of look; that a mother would give her child who was showin-out in front of company. It was *that look* that pierced right through you and wrenched your heart. We were about to lose our dear, sweet Momma. Things would never be the same for us. No matter how hard we tried to justify and even lie to ourselves, the truth was staring us right in the face -- Momma was leaving this old world.

I don't want to remember anymore. It hurts like hell to remember. I mean it really hurts like hell. The pain is sometimes so unbearable. I just want to go to sleep and when I wake, I pray that it'll be all over. I just can't make the memories stop. Please God, make them stop before I lose my mind. Let's see, where was I? Oh yes;

I stood on the side of Momma's bed wiping her brow. She was sweating, something bad. Whatever it was that lived inside of her, it was sure as hell trying its best to get out. If it had to take her life to do so, that's just what it would do.

Sarah rocked back and forth in Momma's old, rickety rocking chair. It had seen many good days - from rocking-to-sleep her grandchildren to her great-grandchildren, to watching the neighborhood children play basketball out back in the school field.

Sarah's eyes never left Momma. Her silence was deafening. If she could, she would leave this world behind too, as long as she could be with her Momma.

I looked over at Sarah again, but this time something was different. *Sarah knew.* She knew what was about to happen.

"You better call the family. I don't think she'll make it through the night," I said to Sarah.

She immediately stopped rocking, as if I had exposed a family secret. We were both in the same room. She had to feel what I was feeling; she had to know what was going on. I didn't want to lose Momma, but whether we wanted to or not, she was going to die.

"Call Shirley and tell her to come home as soon as she can."

Shirley was my middle sister. It was just Sarah, Shirley, and me now.

Buzzy, our only brother, had died unexpectedly... some time ago. It nearly killed Momma. She had to bury one of her own children. A mother's not supposed to bury her child. Children are supposed to outlive their parents.

Shirley had run to the pharmacy, down Ambler, to get Momma's medicine. Although, I think Shirley knew that Momma was beyond the help of medicine. She just had to go.

I think she just needed to get away.

We all had our *roles* in the family. I was the oldest and took responsibility for the care of the sick. I didn't mind the smell of death. I was used to it. So many times I had handed the willing and the unwilling over to death.

Shirley was good at handling the business of the family. She was the educated one. And, dare I say, everyone in the family depended on her to help settle their affairs. She knew what to say and how to say it. Shirley didn't care for the sick, it just wasn't her thing. She did everything else, but the sick, wasn't one of them.

Sarah was the quiet one. She stayed much to herself, but if you needed her, she was always there. She was the spitting image of Momma up and down. She was gentle, kind hearted, and loved her family. Oh yes, she loved her family. The last thing I remembered was Sarah getting up out of the chair and going down the hallway. I could hear each and every step she took. I even heard her step on that one weak piece of flooring that would creek, still to this day.

It was Momma and Daddy's alarm telling them that someone was up and out of their bed when they weren't supposed to be.

I could hear her dialing the phone and breathing heavily. I don't know who she was talking to, but all I could hear her say was, "Gert said Momma's not going to make it through the night. You all better come on up."

After that, I just went blank.

*   *   *   *

Momma had been sick for a number of years. Some say she just woke up one morning and decided that she was tired. She was tired of this weary life and just simply wanted to go on home. If you ask me, I'd tell you that she missed Daddy. He had died long before Momma took real sick. She never was quite the same after his death. I think I wanted to believe that it was Daddy's death that caused Momma to give up. I really wanted to believe this, but I know the truth.

The *truth*? Well, the truth is Momma had cancer. It was eating her up on the inside, leaving in its place a shell of a woman who once was alive and so vibrant. She was beautiful in every way, and now Momma had withered away to nothing. She weighed, at most, eighty pounds soaking wet. Her skin just hung off of her bones. We had to be careful when moving her, 'cause she would scream in pain with every twist and turn. I would tell her so many times, "Momma, I'm almost done. I'm sorry Momma, but I have to change you."

Cancer had taken my mother's dignity away by forcing her to wear diapers. Momma couldn't help herself. She just lost control, and I cleaned her up and made her all better. That's just what I tell myself. I don't know if I made anything better. Regardless of the reason, she fought a good fight and gracefully extended her hand to death and decided to go willingly. I don't know how, or even when, someone comes to that understanding or acceptance to just go willingly. Do they just give up? Or were they just beaten down to the point where it just didn't make any sense to continue fighting knowing that death was going to win? Surrendering with her dignity made it easier on both the family and Momma as well.

She had done her job well and could leave this old world behind without regret. She had prepared her daughters for the harsh conditions and unfair treatment to be handed to them by this cruel world. She shared its beauty with them as well. However, she didn't raise no fools. She wanted her children to be able to stand strong in the face of adversity and remain true to who they are and to the family.

Momma knew that there was no coming back after this last go round. She had prepared for this very moment as best she could. No matter how much it hurts or how painful it was, she wouldn't scream or beg for mercy. She knew that God was watching over her.

* * * *

The smell of death was present in the air. It lingered with a purpose. No matter how many wonderful memories of Momma I clung to, that smell seemed to attach itself to each and every one. I will take that smell to my grave. As the family slowly filled the house, I couldn't help but make peace with it.

On her deathbed, Momma *thanked God* for her life and loving family. She led a good life. She was kind to others...raised her family to the best of her ability... and served the Lord with gladness. Perhaps she was being comforted by the thought of Heaven and all that was promised to her. There would be no more suffering, no more crying, and no more sadness. There would only be peace.

Being the oldest, there were so many understood expectations on me; whether I wanted them or not. I made Momma a promise early on in life: I would be with her up until the very end. Nothing would come in between me and my promise, except death itself. We knew death very well. We were on a first name basis. It hovered over our home. It needed no invitation to stop by. It had been here many times before claiming innocent victim after innocent victim. Death didn't care who you were. When your time was up, it came a knocking.

"Momma, can you hear me? It's Gert," I said.

I waved my hand over Momma's eyes a couple of times. I guess I was hoping for some type of response. I just wanted to know if she was in any pain or if she even knew that I was near.

She never moved. I couldn't move. I stared death right in its eyes. I wasn't going to let it see me break. Momma raised me to be strong. She raised us all to be strong and to carry on. We were not going to break. I didn't want to accept the fact that she was not of this world anymore and that I had no say so in the matter.

I was so caught up in the moment that I never even recognized the faint smell of smoke lingering in the room. My thoughts were interrupted by the sound of the window pane cracking followed by a cool breeze flowing into the room.

It was Shirley. She had returned with Momma's medicine. As I lifted my head and gazed in her eyes, I was greeted by an unfamiliar expression on her face. Shirley was always confident and knew what to say and do to make every situation better. Not this time. Shirley stood by the window smoking a cigarette. She only smoked Marlboro Lights. Why I remembered that, I don't know, but it was true. As she took a drag, she held the smoke in for a little bit. She always said it calmed her nerves. With one gentle breath, she turned her head and blew the smoke out the window. She didn't immediately turn back to look at me or Momma. She gazed out the window and looked to the Heavens. She just stared longingly into the night. By this time, the storm had passed...the stars shined brightly, as the moon lit up the night's sky. There was a sense of calmness in the air. This was the time when she had to choose whether or not to continue to believe in all that she was taught in church.

Although she didn't understand why God had chosen this night on this particular day to take her mother, she continued to trust in Him and His Word. She asked herself quietly, "Is there really a God?"

No one wanted to ask the forbidden question, but they thought it to themselves. She relied on her faith to heal her broken heart and to answer her many unanswered questions. This family never questioned the will of the Lord. God's will was perfect or was it? Shirley couldn't bear looking at her Momma lying in her bed. This was not the mother that she knew and loved. Who was this shell of a woman in front of her?

"*Mom*...Mom, it's me Shirley. Can you hear me? I know you're tired. You've raised your family and if you want to go on home and rest, it's o.k. We'll be fine. *We'll be just fine.* Momma it's o.k. to go-on-home and be with Daddy now."

By this time, Sarah had returned to the bedroom and sat back in Momma's rocking chair. She wanted to call out, to shout, to scream, and even to curse God for taking her mother; but she remained silent. Remaining silent was safe. In silence, she talked with Momma. She would miss her more than she would ever be able to convey. It was a moment, uninterrupted by the world. How could God be so uncaring? How could an all-powerful God permit such an injustice to take place? Did He even care? Did anyone care? If she didn't hold onto the memory of her mother, then who would ever remember her? The world would just go on as if nothing had ever happened. They would forget Momma.

The stillness in the room was soon replaced by an unsettling sound. Death was close by. My family called this sound the death rattles. It ushered in and announced the presence of death itself.

"Momma, what's wrong? Do you want something?" Sarah asked.

All Momma could do was move ever so slightly in the bed. She appeared to be trying to say something to her three daughters, but was unable to. She shook her head back and forth and stared out the window. Something was pulling her away from us. Momma tried to raise up in the bed, but was so weak. She lifted her arms to the sky and stretched her hands out. We all gathered around the bed and held hands. The time had come.

I looked at Shirley, "Give it to me. I'll do it."

"No Gert, you don't have to."

"Give it to me! Please, not now." As the rattles grew louder, Shirley reached behind her and grabbed the brown paper bag. She was reluctant to hand it over to me, but she knew what had to be done. "It's okay," I said.

I reached inside the bag and pulled out the syringe. "The doctor said to put this on Momma's neck when the rattles started." I tried being brave, but it was no use. We all began to weep. We knew that it was just a matter of time before Momma would pass. Somehow this medicine would make things easier on us and Momma. It was supposed to stop the rattles. To this day, I can still hear that eerie sound. It haunts me in my sleep. I can't forget that sound.

"Gert," Shirley said as I squeezed the medicine onto Momma's neck.

"Yes?"

"Don't...don't forget to put on the gloves. I remember the doctor telling us to wear gloves." Shirley seemed so cold and distant as she talked. I didn't hate her for reminding me, but wanted to lash out. I wanted to scream at the top of my lungs and blame someone for all the pain inside of me. I would just be taking it out on her because she was here. How could you be so distant? This was Momma that we were talking about. This was the woman who raised us and protected us. I had to remind myself that Shirley was right. No matter how it was said or taken, she was right.

"Yeah...thanks," I said as I put both gloves on. It killed me to have to put on gloves to touch my Momma. As I began rubbing the medicine into her neck, the rattles slowly faded away. It was only a matter of minutes before Momma looked around the room; smiled at her daughters and quietly closed her eyes.

She had such a pleasant look on her face. Momma took in one shallow breath and slowly fell limp in the bed. Her hand gently fell off the side of the bed and hung lifelessly. She was gone. Momma was gone. Once again death had come quietly in the middle of the night to steal the breath of another loved one.

"Momma!" I shouted. "Don't leave us. Please don't leave us."

I reached down and lifted Momma's hand placing it back on the side of the bed. Shirley quietly bent over Momma and laid her head in the center of her chest soaking her nightgown with her tears. She screamed out, "She's gone Gert! She's gone!"

Sarah walked back to the rocking chair and quietly folded her hands in her lap. She wanted to forget this moment. She wanted to forget everything. She wanted things to be as they were before. It was a selfish thought, that Sarah just didn't want to have to experience and feel. No, she didn't want her mother to suffer anymore and understood that she was in a better place. Her spirit had been lifted and she was now free.

"No more pain Momma. No more suffering! You're free!" I cried.

It was during this time that we all reflected on past memories of Momma. All that was left behind was a sisterhood; a bond that was now made stronger and fortified by death. The times to come would test the strength of our relationship, faith in God, and determination to survive.

Shirley broke away from the mourning and immediately began taking the lead in making the funeral arrangements.

"I'll call Ciavarelli and let him know that Momma has passed." The Ciavarellis owned a very successful funeral home in the Ambler area. From the time I could remember, they were the only funeral home that this family ever used. They didn't care about the color of your skin or the money in your pocket. They worked with you. They were like family.

"Don't forget to call Reverend Jones. Maybe he'll come by

tonight and say a prayer for the family," I requested.

Reverend Jones was the pastor of our church, Bethlehem Baptist Church. He was that old-time, Baptist preacher. He sure knew how to deliver a sermon with that fire and brimstone in his voice. He made you feel God's presence.

The church would be swaying and the choir would be singing to sounds of hand clapping. Fans waved back and forth, the good old days; I would give anything for the good old days again.

"Oh yeah, that's right. I will have to check with him to see when the church is available. So many people have died in the last couple of weeks," Shirley answered. Shirley knew what had to be done and she did it. Emotions would only get in the way. She did not have time to allow her feelings to slow her down and interfere with the process of making the arrangements. Sarah and I were the emotional ones. It was not a question of right or wrong, fair or unfair, that's just the way things were done. Everyone had their responsibility and job to do. As Shirley stepped out of the room, I began cleaning Momma up. I washed her face, brushed her hair, and changed her clothes. I know, I know. What difference did it make? Well, it made a whole lot of difference to me. I just couldn't let them see Momma any old kind of way.

*   *   *   *

Sarah quietly walked downstairs to let the family know that Momma had passed. Their long anticipation was finally over. Soon, family members gathered in the room and around the bed to pay their last respects to a mother, grandmother, great-grandmother, and aunt. As the family, friends, and neighbors flowed throughout the house, we never left the side of our mother. I continued to sit by Momma rubbing her hands and gently touching her face.

"She looks so peaceful," I said to myself.

Somehow, the look on Momma's face made her death somewhat bearable. Time seemed to pass so quickly. Hours seemed like minutes. Minutes seemed like seconds. I don't know how long I had been sitting beside Momma, but it seemed like an eternity.

Soon there was a knock on the front door. It was the funeral home and Reverend Jones coming to remove the body. Although this was an unsettling feeling for the family, especially for Sarah, they knew that it had to be done. We all followed the sound of the footsteps climbing the rickety staircase, down the hallway, and stopping at the bedroom door. Reluctantly, we looked up and greeted the Reverend, Mr. Ciavarelli, and his sons. To me, it felt like losing her all over again. Sarah quietly turned her head from the window and took in one last look of Momma.

"Thank you for coming so quickly. Before you take her, Reverend, would you please say a word of prayer over Momma?" Shirley asked.

As Reverend Jones approached the bed, he placed his black, brimmed hat on the night stand beside Momma's bed. He shook the hand of each sister and said, "She lived a good life. It was truly an honor to know your mother. I thank God for our precious moments shared and truly thank Him for this family."

"Thank you Reverend," Shirley replied. "she was very fond of you."

Reverend Jones began to pray. "Now, if you all don't mind, let us now join hands and bow our heads for a moment of prayer.

Dear Heavenly Father, tonight we call upon your
name asking for a word of comfort. Come by here oh
Lord and bless this family right now. They are in need

of healing; for we know that you are all powerful and
can ease all broken hearts and uplift the wounded
soul. In their time of need, dear Heavenly Father, be
with them. Reassure them that you are present and
have not left them. For we know that Mrs. Smith is
resting in your arms. Now please let your light shine
in the midst of darkness and be with the Smith family
now and forever more. Amen."

Once Reverend Jones finished his prayer, we just stood there holding hands. No one wanted to be the first to let go. Letting go would only quicken the removal of Momma's body. I think I was the first to drop my hands, then Shirley. Sarah...well, she grabbed Momma's hand and just stared at her. She didn't cry or scream. She just stood there. I tried pulling her back from the bed, but she refused to move.

"Sarah," I quietly whispered into her ear. "Let go honey."

"I'm not leaving! I can't leave her. She wouldn't leave us and you know that, Gert."

Sarah was right. Momma wouldn't leave any of us.

"Sarah, are you sure?" asked Shirley.

"You don't want this to be the last memory you have of Momma."

"Yes, I'm sure!"

As difficult as it was, I just couldn't get myself to leave either. How could I watch them take my Momma, put her in a bag, zip her up, and haul her off like she was nothing? I kept on reminding myself that there was no other way. This wasn't going to be easy on any of us.

"I'm not leaving either, Shirley. I told Momma that I would be with her until the end and that's what I'm going to do."

"Fine, then we will *all* stay," agreed Shirley.

As Reverend Jones walked the remaining family members

out of the bedroom, he glanced back at the three of us gathered around Momma's bedside. It was a touching sight. Soon, the two sons lifted Momma's lifeless body off the bed and gently placed her in a black bag.

I just remember hollering at the top of my lungs, "Momma! Don't take my Momma from me! Please God, don't take my Momma from me!"

Shirley grabbed my side, as I hunched over, begging God to give Momma back to me. I couldn't believe that the woman who raised us our entire life was gone, in what seemed to be in a matter of minutes.

"Lawd no! Please Lawd, no!" Sarah shouted as she fell back into the rocking chair. Shirley fanned Sarah as she held onto me. She was a rock; or at least it seemed on the outside.

It was too much. I thought I was strong enough, but Lord I was wrong. I just continued to holler, "Momma! Momma! Momma!"

I soon felt the comforting touch of Reverend Jones' hand on my shoulder.

"Gertrude, breathe. I need for you to breathe for me."

I couldn't catch my breath. I tried over and over again and just couldn't catch my breath. Reverend Jones guided me out the bedroom door to the front room where he sat me on the side of the bed.

"No! No! Please let me stay. I'll be fine. Please!"

Shirley stayed with Sarah and saw to it that Momma was taken care of. As Momma was carried out of the house, I could hear other family members screaming and pleading to God. "No, no, not Nana!"

"Nana, don't leave us!"

"God no! Bring her back! Bring her back to us! Please!"

No amount of begging or pleading would change the fact that Momma was gone and never coming back. How were we supposed to just move on without her? It just didn't seem fair. I didn't want to forget what cancer did to my Momma. I wasn't going to let the world act as if nothing had happened and wake up the next morning and go about their daily lives. I didn't know what I was going to do, but I was going to do something.

For now, I had to learn how to live *without* Momma. I was going to need my sisters more than ever.

*   *   *   *

Soon, the house was silent. Funny, people seem to always leave you when you need them the most. It's not during the dying that you need family and friends around, it's after everything is said and done. You need their sound and presence to fill up the silence. As I looked around the house, I only saw Sarah still sitting in the back room rocking. I thought it best that I just give her a moment to herself. I didn't know where Shirley was, but all I had to do was follow the faint smell of smoke coming from downstairs. She must be stressed. As I walked down the stairs, I saw my sister sitting at the dining room table with Momma and Daddy's papers spread out. Shirley had already started planning the funeral.

"The church is free this coming Saturday and the Reverend said we could have the service then."

Shirley didn't even turn around to look at me.

"Shirley-"

"I thought that we could go to the funeral home sometime tomorrow and bring her clothes and finish up the funeral arrangements."

"Shirley-"

"Momma loved pink. I'll bring her pink dress and...oh yes, we'll have to get pink slippers too and-"

"Shirley!"

Shirley dropped her hand and placed her cigarette in the

ashtray. All I could do was hold my sister. I held her in my arms as I brushed her hair back. She needed me but would never say it. I respected her strength and willingness to put on this impenetrable façade, but I knew that underneath was my little sister just wanting to be held.

"Shirley, I'm here if you need to-"

"I'm fine Gert. I just needed...well, thanks."

Shirley pushed away from the table and gathered her belongings.

"Sarah...Sissy I'm gone," She yelled upstairs.

Soon Sarah joined us downstairs at the front door. We didn't know what to say to each other, so we simply hugged and smiled. Shirley and Sarah left out the house and walked to their cars not saying a word to each other. It was late. It must have been 3:00 am or so. No one was stirring in the streets. As Shirley and Sarah drove off, I simply turned the porch light off, shut the door, and silently cried to myself. As I looked around the empty house, it hit me like a ton of bricks, "God, I'm alone."

*   *   *   *

The week before the funeral was a blur. There were so many people coming in and out of the house; leaving cards, sharing their condolences. Sometimes just sitting quietly with me. The days seemed to go by so quickly. Before I knew it, I was sitting in my bedroom, Momma's old room, staring at my clothes spread out across the bed. I don't remember taking them out or even deciding on what to wear. My mind is so full and heavy that sometimes I just feel like I was going to have a nervous breakdown.

Tradition in our family concerning funeral services was very simple. The immediate family all gathered the morning of the funeral at the main house, Momma's house. The men rose that morning before everyone and made sure that all the cars that were to be a part of the procession had been washed and cleaned out. Sometime around 10:30 am, we all gathered downstairs and prayed for the Lord's blessings and comfort. Around 10:45 am, we left the house and drove to the church. Just like clockwork, we arrived in front of the church with ten minutes to spare. The church was just down the hill from our house. We could have walked if we wanted to. It was not until 11:00am did we exit the cars. Other family members were lined-up outside the church, awaiting our arrival. Most, if not all, of the community and friends of the family had already been seated in the church.

Tradition dictated that Momma be funeralized at Bethlehem Baptist Church. This was the church that we all grew up in and served. It was here at Bethlehem where Shirley conducted the children's choir, the Sun Beams, and Daddy held the position of Head Deacon. Reverend Jones had delivered many powerful and inspirational sermons from the pulpit encouraging his congregation to live *good Christian lives*. In our family, funerals were not a time to mourn. This was a time to celebrate and to be thankful for the gift of life. Although tears would flow and the question "why" would be asked, the saving grace for the family was our faith in knowing that we would all be reunited one glad morning. This was only a temporary parting. Life everlasting was promised. As Shirley, Sarah, and I sat in the limousine, so many thoughts ran through my mind. I wanted to yell out Momma's name as loudly as I could, but it would only be in vain. Momma's not coming back. So instead, I just sat there staring out the window. I really wasn't looking at anything in particular. I just wanted an escape. It's hard to believe that she's gone. For the past four years or so, my entire life has been dedicated to caring for Momma.

I would first get myself together early in the morning; then run her bath water, bathe and dress her, comb her hair, and then fix her breakfast. I couldn't go anywhere since Momma needed around-the-clock care.

Just the thought of not having to take care of Momma anymore brought tears to my eyes. Although I didn't want to admit it, I was somewhat relieved. The stress had been getting to me.

"What am I going to do with my life now?" I questioned out loud.

"What are we all going to do now?" Shirley said. "We all spent the last couple of years taking care of Momma."

"Shirley, I wasn't saying that you and Sarah didn't care for Momma or that I cared for her more than you all. It's just-"

"Gert, I know that's not what you meant. Sissy, we all are going to miss her. Somehow, we just have to find a way to move on."

The thought of moving on without Momma sickened me. How do you just move on as if Momma never existed? She was a person... a real, living, breathing person and I have to move on? It's just not right. "It's just...I'll never be able to comb her hair anymore. She's gone Shirley." There was nothing no one could say to me to make the situation better. My sisters just gave me permission to feel. They didn't attempt to calm me or to stop me from feeling. They remained quiet as I just sat in my feelings. I glanced over at Sarah sitting across from me. She was so distant. I felt the strong urge to lash out at her to make her react to something. She just sat there hiding behind her sunglasses, not moving, and appearing to be unaffected by all that was going on around her. I knew this wasn't the case, but I just needed to see or hear some type of reaction. I guess I was the one with the problem. It just wouldn't be fair to lash out at her when I'm sure she was mourning herself. However, before I knew it, I had called out her name.

"Sarah-"

"No, Gert. Please not now." She wasn't as distant as I thought. Sarah was right there in the midst of all the pain and despair that we all were feeling. She was raw and vulnerable like us all. Without warning, a knock on the tinted window was heard and soon was followed by the door opening and a hand reaching inside the car. "Ms. Gertrude, Ms. Shirley, Ms. Sarah, may I help you out?" The driver of the limousine had extended his hand inside the car anticipating a welcomed reception. No one moved. No one talked. We just stared at each other and then at the youthful hand. Someone would have to be the first to make contact. Without further hesitation, Shirley reached out. One by one, we all slowly filed out the car. What seemed to be an eternity was only a matter of ten minutes. As my eyes adjusted to the sun's blinding light beaming directly on us announcing our arrival, I soon was able to recognize familiar faces affixed on us. I thought to myself, "How are we going to survive without her?"

As we were being escorted to the front of the processional line, I found comfort in the familiar faces greeting me as I passed by. I was unstable on my feet and several times lost my footing. With each step, I fought back my tears and seemed to grow weaker and weaker. As we reached the front of the line, I focused on a familiar sight-the church's red doors. Sunday after Sunday we were ushered into the church through the familiar red doors and thought nothing of it. However, today was different. The doors seemed to taunt me over and over. Make them stop. Please make them stop. Once we entered through the doors, we would never be the same.

"Oh Shirley, I don't think I'm going to be able to do it."

"Yes, you can and will."

"I can't move."

"You will be fine. We will all be fine. We have each other."

Soon the doors to the church opened and the family was greeted by a familiar sound. It was my youngest son, Bradie. He was singing for his grandmother. No music accompanied him, just the sound of a slow, steady foot hitting the hardwood floors. As the family proceeded into the church, I focused on my son's voice. He stood in the pulpit with his eyes closed and hands outstretched as he sang. Bradie was singing his Nana to Heaven.

"Done made my vow to the Lord and
I never will turn back. I will go.
0 I shall go to see what the end will be."

- *"Done Made My Vow" by John Wesley Work, Jr.*

As he sang, tears streamed down his face. The pulse of the song was slow and steady. You could hear soulful moans and *lifted praises*, as bodies bowed in anticipation of the Lord's arrival.

"Sing, baby. Sing."

As we climbed the last step leading into the church, we were greeted by Reverend Jones. His presence was reassuring. As he gazed across the faces of each family member, a sense of peace fell upon us.

"Your mother would be so proud of you all. Weep not for her, for she is with God."

Gonna serve my Lord while I have breath. To see what the end will be. So I can serve Him after death. To see what the end will be. - *"Done Made My Vow" by John Wesley Work, Jr.*

"Please stand and receive the family," Reverend Jones announced to the congregation. As the congregation stood, we began to slowly walk down the aisle of the church. I could hear the wailing of each family member as we passed by. Shirley, Sarah, and I walked arm and arm down the aisle. I was afraid, but pretended to be strong. I just reminded myself to focus on Bradie.

Done made my vow to the Lord and I never will turn back. I will go. I shall go to see what the end will be.

As the family passed by the casket, things became blurry to me. I could hear Bradie in the background singing, but everything else around me blended in together. Some family members passed silently by placing a hand on the casket, while others threw their arms up screaming to the rafters of the church.

"Why Lord? Why did you have to take her? Not Nana. Not Nana," shouted a grandchild.

Gonna pray and pray and never stop. To see what the end will be. Until I reach the mountain top. To see what the end will be. Done made my vow to the Lord and I never will turn back.

I will go.

I shall go to see what the end will be.

- *"Done Made My Vow" by John Wesley Work, Jr.*

I needed for Bradie to continue singing. I found refuge in the music. Truth be told, I really needed it because it prolonged the inevitable. I dreaded what was to come next. As the song ended, we took our seats in front of the congregation facing the casket.

I never really thought about how difficult this must have been for my son. Ever since the family realized he could sing, he was asked to sing at all the funerals and weddings in the community. Never saying no, Bradie just focused on what needed to be done and he did it. He was so young to have to deal with such pain and sorrow. As he took his seat beside me, he quietly buried his head in my lap. I shielded him from being seen. I had to protect him.

The organist underpinned the silence with *There's a Sweet, Sweet Spirit,* quietly in the background. As Reverend Jones rose to his feet, we all understood what was about to take place.

"Gertrude, Shirley, Sarah, it's time to say your last goodbyes."

Inside, I cursed God for this very moment. I cursed Him for putting my family through such turmoil. How could He do this to us? As we reached down to our sides, we simultaneously clasped hands and squeezed ever so tightly. With each pulse, we drew upon each other's strength.

Sarah was the first to approach the casket. As her hand lifelessly dropped to her side, she closed her eyes forcefully and shook her head as if attempting to wake from a nightmare. It seemed like just yesterday, when she was sitting on the front porch with Momma rocking back and forth on the glider. That day was perfect. Life was good.

"Sarah, be brave," I whispered as she walked to the casket.

Sarah appeared to be jarred back into reality by the sound of my voice. As she reached the head of the casket, the congregation joined the organist as the *Hymn of Praise* was sung. Soon the church was filled again with praise and worship.

Sarah just stared at Momma. She took everything in; the salt and pepper color of her hair, the peaceful expression on her face, the beautiful pink gown she was wearing, and the satin slippers on her feet. Sarah lowered her head and softly kissed Momma on her forehead. No matter how hard she tried to focus on the belief that her mother was in a better place, she couldn't help but acknowledge and to accept her anger and resentment towards God for taking her mother away from her, in the first place. Why did *He* let her suffer as she did and for so long?

Before returning to her seat, Sarah whispered into her mother's ear. It was a special message only to be heard by and shared with her Momma.

"Goodbye Momma. I will never forget you."

I couldn't help but notice how Sarah seemed so drained. Her gait was even that of a different person. She was hunched over as she walked, lethargically back to her seat. She was void of emotion and expression. This wasn't my sister.

I was next to share a private moment with Momma. I felt the overwhelming urge to hold my dear sister, encourage and strengthen her. It's funny how certain things affix themselves to your memory. I can still smell the perfume that Sarah wore that day. It was soft and sweet as a summer afternoon. It soothed me. I reached out towards Sarah, as she walked effortlessly into my embrace. Her breathing was labored. I could feel her heart pounding through her chest. In public, I always pretended to be impenetrable and unaffected by the world around me. The truth is I wasn't. I hurt and feel. I guarded my feelings to protect my heart; however, at this very moment, I didn't care who saw or took advantage of my pain. I sobbed like a newborn baby being separated from her mother for the first time. I was supposed to be tough. Nothing was supposed to get next to me. I was the fighter and protector of others. I had never encountered a situation like this before in my life. I never came across such an overpowering feeling of sadness. It tore at my gut and was unrelenting. It was a moment that would stay with me for the rest of my life, but prepared me for tomorrow's anguish. As I reached the casket, I cried out.

"Momma!" I could not find the strength to utter another word. I was so weak. Breathing became a conscious effort. Who was I going to care for now? I prided myself on taking care of my family. It was my purpose. It was my calling. I was good at it and everyone knew to call on Gert in times of need. It's funny how I remember certain things on that day; strange, unimportant things, but I remember. It took me four steps to walk from Sarah to Momma's casket. Four steps. Why do I remember that? Once at the casket, I softly rubbed Momma's hands again and again. "I'm a miss you very much, Momma." With my last ounce of strength, I walked back and locked eyes on Shirley. The next thing I remember was the ushers rushing to my side escorting me back to my seat. What happened? I was told later that I had collapsed. As the ushers fanned me and loosened the collar to my blouse, Shirley remained the pillar of strength. She was always in control of her emotions, her thoughts, and the situation. She accepted the death of Momma as factual and inevitable. Shirley understood life's process; we are born, live, and then die. This was never going to change. She accepted death and didn't fear it. Perhaps in her private moments she questioned the acts of God, but never allowed herself to lose sight of the truth of the matter. We would never live forever. Shirley stood over the casket beaming. She was proud to gaze upon such a remarkable creation. This was her mother and she adored her. Yes, she would miss her, but she was thankful for the time that God allowed Momma to be in her life. "Momma, you did a great job raising us. Rest and know that we will be alright."

Shirley slowly returned back to her seat; smiled at the sight of all Momma's family and friends biding her a fond farewell.

As we stood tightly nestled together, two men dressed in black suits, white, starched shirts, and black ties walked from the corners of the church and stood on either side of the casket. I hated what was about to happen. They call themselves shielding us, buffering us from the sight of Momma being lowered into the casket, but it didn't work. I could see her slowly disappearing deeper into the casket. I could see everything.

"Momma!" I screamed "Momma! Don't take my Momma!"

I know it was hard on everyone, but everyone was not my concern. This was all about me and my feelings.

"Oh, God please don't take her. I'll do anything, just please don't take her!" pleaded Sarah.

Shirley lowered her head slightly as she shut her eyes and wrapped her arms around us. It was too much for everyone, even for Shirley. The two men pulled the silk blanket up over Momma stopping just short of her face and then lowered her deeper into the casket. I know they were aware that we were standing right behind them and could see everything. I didn't want to hate them, but I did. I wanted to blame someone that was tangible. I needed the satisfaction due to me by someone just listening and accepting the blame, the fault, and my hatred. I hated cancer for continuously disrupting my life and hurting the people I love. The two men cautiously lowered the top to the casket and placed a colorful flower arrangement on top. I can't hate them, but I do. The church fell silent. We were all then presented with one flower from the arrangement as the two men disappeared into the recesses of the church.

I don't know how they managed to pull themselves together after such an outcry of emotions, but Wendy, Sarah's daughter, and Georgie, Shirley's son, rose from their seats and approached the pulpit. Their grandmother would be so proud of them.

"We will be reading from the Old Testament, Psalm 23," announced Georgie.

"The Lord is my shepherd; I shall not want. He maketh me to lie down in green pastures. He leadeth me beside the still waters. He restoreth my soul. He leadeth me in the paths of righteousness for His name sake. Yea, though I walk through the valley of the shadow of death, I will fear no evil: for thou art with me; thy rod and thy staff they comfort me. Thou prepareth a table before me in the presence of mine enemies: thou anointest my head with oil; my cup runneth over. Surely goodness and mercy shall follow me all the days of my life: and I will dwell in the house of the Lord forever. Amen."

"Amen," the family repeated.

As Wendy and Georgie took their seats, Reverend Jones approached the podium. He stood tall, erect, and confident. As he peered out over the congregation, a sense of tranquility entered my heart. It was almost over and I accepted it. The most difficult part of the service was behind us now. I relaxed back in the pew and focused on the trance-like timbre of the Reverend's voice.

"In keeping with the wishes of the family, my words will be brief. To the family of Mrs. Helen Smith, I wish to extend my deepest, heartfelt condolences. It is truly a pleasure to stand in the presence of such a remarkable family. Month after month and year after year, I have watched your struggle and continue to be amazed by your courage, strength, and conviction. You are the epitome of family unity. I pray that God continues to stand beside you in your time of need and comfort you when your burdens are heavy laden. Know that God is ever present, all powerful, and can calm your raging sea. Call on Him in your midnight hour, for He hears and answers all prayers. Let us pray."

As Reverend Jones prayed for continued healing, strength, and God's favor over the family, the church began to worship - bodies rocking; fans waved feverishly; hands clapped to the rhythmic pulse of the Reverend's sermon; and voices raised praises to Heaven above. Family members who were slain in the spirit were encircled by the ushers who prayed for God Himself to move through the building.

"Have your way, Lord. Have your way," exalted the Head Usher.

We were safe. Old and young were being touched by the word of God. The vamps from the musicians accented the strained inflections of the Pastor. The choir stood and rocked back and forth, swaying to the music. Reverend Jones raised his hands and prayed like he never prayed before.

"Many who bow before you today, Lord, with heavy and sorrow filled hearts, are in deep mourning, Lord. Some, dear Heavenly Father, come with anger and hurt in their hearts; while others come with a sense of hopelessness and despair. Yet others come with an unwavering faith and find comfort in your word. Lord, this family is under attack. How much longer will this family be under siege, Lord? How much longer will this family have to endure such turmoil? Day after day, week after week, and month after month this family sits by and watches their loved ones being abruptly taken away from them. How much longer will this unyielding, uncaring, and seemingly all powerful spirit be permitted to snipe the very life out of your children and go unpunished?" The church was in an uproar by this point. Some Deacons stood in front of the pulpit and echoed the words being delivered by the Pastor.

"Yes, Pastor! Preach on Pastor!"

"When Dear Heavenly Father will enough be enough? We stand and declare that today...yes this day that the Lord has made will be the day that this family takes back all that the enemy has stolen from them. We, your children ban together and take back every ounce of hurt and pain that was ripped away from us. We will no longer be voluntary victims of our circumstances. No longer will we bow in humble submission. No longer will we go willingly into the lion's den-"

"Preach Pastor! Amen!" joined in one of the Deaconesses.

"We will fight with every fiber of our being. We rally together and declare war on the enemy. Devil, you are being served your final eviction notice! You have no more power here, Demon. Let all within the sound of my voice shout halleluiah... halleluiah, and Amen!"

Momma would have said, "That sermon was good to her."

Reverend Jones rocked back and forth as he shook his hands

27

in an attempt to regain his composure.

"Yes Lord. Thank you, Lord. You've been so good to us. We're not worthy, Lord. You've been so good to us. Thank you, Lord. Thank you."

Reverend Jones slowly raised his hands in the air and stated, "May all within the sound of my voice stand and prepare for the benediction. The Lord bless thee and keep thee. The Lord make his face to shine upon thee, and be gracious unto thee. The Lord lift his countenance upon thee, and give thee peace. Amen."

As the flower girls began to file one by one into the aisle, each took a floral arrangement from the altar and recessed-out the church. The pall bearers followed next. Simultaneously, the casket was lifted and carried to the rear of the church. As the congregation exited, Brad stood and began singing.

> *Guide my feet. While I run this race.*
> *Oh Lord, guide my feet, while I run this race.*
> *Yes, guide my feet, while I run this race.*
> *For I don't want to run this race in vain, race in vain.*
> *Pray for me. While I run this race.*
> *Lord, pray for me. While I run this race.*
> *Yes, pray for me. While I run this race.*
> *For I don't want to run this race in vain.*
> *Race in vain.*

-*"Guide My Feet" African American Spiritual, Composer Unknown*

As Shirley, Sarah and I reached the back of the church, we stopped just a few feet shy of the red doors. We joined hands as we gazed back into the sanctuary. It was over. We had survived. Or did we? "Rest in peace Momma."

CHAPTER TWO

The Repass

Momma was laid to rest at Rose Valley Cemetery. She was finally reunited with the love of her life, Daddy. Although he had died some years before Momma, she always dreamed of this very day, where she would rest in the arms of *her* Phillip again. Somehow, the thought of Daddy and Momma embracing each other brought a smile to my face.

"It sure must have been a beautiful sight," I said to myself.

"What?" Shirley asked as she turned to face me in the back of the limousine.

"Momma and Daddy holding each other, after being apart for such a long time."

"Can you imagine? The thought of it just brings tears to my eyes."

As the limousine entered the small community of Penllyn, I gazed out the tinted window and took one last glance at Bethlehem Baptist Church. It was hard to believe that we were just there about an hour ago saying goodbye to Momma.

I was tired. We all were tired. Funerals just drained the life out of you. I just wanted to go home and be alone. I didn't want any company or forced conversations. No one knew what to say or do, so they just said anything and did anything that came to mind. It never made you feel any better or took away any of the pain, but you appreciated the effort.

"How are we going to move on with our lives?" Sarah quietly asked.

The voice was faint and almost unrecognizable. Sarah never moved or indicated to whom she was directing her question. Despite appearing to be so emotionally distant, she was very present and aware of all that was going on around her. She sighed, as she gently wiped a single tear streaming down her face.

"I can't believe it. She really is gone," She continued.

I didn't have the energy to cry anymore and didn't want my lack of emotional presence to come across as being uncaring or cold, but I just didn't have it in me. Hell, I didn't even have an answer to her question. The only thing that I could think of to do was simply reach my hand out and place it on top of hers. Her hand was so warm and soft. My mind immediately remembered how Momma's hand felt. It was different.

As the limousine approached the top of the hill of Trewellyn Avenue, we began to gather our things. Shirley slid forward as she tried to slip her shoes back on.

"My feet are swollen."

We couldn't help but laugh. We knew that Shirley didn't like wearing heels and before the day was over, she would have started complaining about her feet hurting and being swollen.

"Nobody told you to wear those shoes in the first place," I said as the car came to a stop in front of the house.

"And nobody asked you for your *two cents* either," Shirley snipped back.

"Well, regardless, here your slippers. Put them on."

"Thanks, Sissy."

We may have our moments sometimes, but just as quickly as they came, they leave.

As is tradition in the family, after a burial, all returned to the main house to participate in the repast. Here, the family shared fond memories, cried again, and ate a home cooked meal. There usually was some form of green beans, macaroni and cheese, salad, fried chicken, deviled eggs, cranberry sauce, sweet tea, and a pound cake made by one of the older ladies in the community. There was no exception to this tradition. Whether you wanted to attend or not, you paid your respect to the grieving family.

Penllyn, Pennsylvania was a small town where everyone knew your name. A place where you could leave your front door open all night and not have to worry about unwanted guests. What you did have to worry about was everyone knowing and getting into your business. That's just how small towns are. We fought, argued, and cursed each other out, but we were still family. One week you spoke to each other and the next you didn't.

Bradie and I had moved back home about two years ago to care for Momma. My Fred had since passed away from complications from his emphysema, so we packed our belongings up and moved back. It was the right thing to do. Bradie was about to go to college and Momma needed caring for. Shirley and Sarah had their lives and families and I couldn't carry the apartment on my own with what I was making, so it just made sense to come back home.

The house was arranged just as Momma had left it and it would remain this way long after her death. As we approached the front door, we could hear the roar of laughter and noise, doors slamming, and silverware clanking as the family settled into their normal routines. I didn't want to deal with all this mess. I wasn't a fan of company and sure as hell didn't like people in my house that on any normal day wouldn't even part their lips to say "hello." That's not how I am. I wasn't fake and didn't like fake people.

Shirley could sense a change in me. She was more rational in times like these than I could ever possibly be.

"Gert, I know. I know. Please hold it together for the sake of Momma."

"Shirley, Sissy, you know me. You better keep an eye on me 'cause if the wrong person says the wrong thing to me-"

"They won't."

Before entering the house, we noticed that Sarah wasn't standing right beside us. "Sarah? Sarah?" both Shirley and I called out.

In the distant background we recognized a familiar sound. It was the glider on the front porch. It always needed oiling, but we couldn't get none of the boys in the family to do so. *Some good they are*. As Sarah rocked back and forth on the white, metal glider, she stared endlessly into space.

"Sarah-", I attempted to call out.

"I'm fine. I just need some time to myself. I'll be in a little later."

Shirley began walking towards Sarah.

"No. Please, I just need some time."

Shirley stopped, with Sarah's subtle warning and smiled.

"Okay. If you need us honey, we'll-"

The glider swayed to a halt, as Sarah turned her head away from us and towards the Johnson's front yard.

"Thanks."

I nudged Shirley as I opened the front door.

"She'll be fine."

As the door swung open, all eyes fell upon us. The family wanted to continue on with their laughter and celebration, but out of respect for us, they didn't. The house was full of friends, neighbors, out-of-town relatives, and children.

As I peered around the living room as far as my eyes could

see, I found myself becoming overwhelmed by the sight. Things were in total disarray and no one appeared to notice or even care. I was neat. I took care of my possessions, as did Momma. I kept my house in order. I couldn't stand things being out of place. As I felt my heart racing, I found myself gasping for air. Shirley knew what was happening. She tried to get my attention, but I couldn't focus on her voice.

"Gertrude? Gert, what's wrong?"

I needed something familiar to give me direction.

It was awkward standing there with so many eyes on me and my eyes on them. No one moved or spoke. I couldn't take it anymore.

"Lord help me. This place is a mess." I immediately began walking through the house picking up glasses and plates that were placed on my good furniture, Momma's furniture. This would have never happened if Momma was alive and it sure as hell won't happen after she's gone. If I have any say in the matter, and I do, I was going to keep things as close to the way as they used to be. I immediately began sweeping through the house, picking-up cups and saucers, crumbled-up napkins and discarded, opened envelopes as well as dirty dishes. I didn't care if they were done with them or not - the house was a mess and I needed something to do.

I needed something to take my mind off the thoughts starting to flood back into my consciousness. Perhaps I was overreacting, but that's just me. They would get over it, as I had already done so.

Soon the house was filled with noise and movement again. Shirley smiled to herself as she closed the door and greeted family that had traveled from out-of-state for Momma's service. "Aunt Florence, you said that you were coming. Momma loved you so much. It's good to see you."

Shirley was good. She was really good at interacting and

mingling and conversing with others. As she moved her way through the living room and into the dining room, she found a seat, her favorite seat by the window. Her ashtray was still sitting on the windowsill, with old cigarette butts piled up on top of each other. I knew they were hers, because I could see the faint traces of lipstick around their edges. Shirley quietly lit a cigarette, took a long drag... and exhaled a thick puff of smoke. All I could do was continue cleaning. Shirley had her cigarettes and I had my cleaning.

"Momma sure looked beautiful," I said as I picked up Shirley's ashtray and dumped its contents into one of the dirty dishes I had resting on my forearm.

I don't even think Shirley realized that she was still carrying her heels in her left hand. Once I placed her ashtray back on the windowsill, I smiled as I stared at the slightly-worn shoes, dangling by their straps.

"Are you gonna carry those around all day?" I asked, pointing to the shoes. Shirley finally realized how silly she looked smoking a cigarette and holding onto her shoes like someone was going to steal them from her. As she dropped the shoes to the floor, she laughed out loud.

"I don't see how y'all can wear these things. My feet are killing me. Child, just give me a plain old pair of flats and I'm good."

I couldn't help but smile and join in on the laughter.

As Shirley relaxed back into the chair, she pulled another puff from the cigarette, the smile slowly disappearing from her face.

"Yes indeed, she did. I tell you, she looked just like she was sleeping."

I didn't know what to say.

Momma wasn't sleeping. She would never wake up. She was gone. Shirley never stopped staring out the window. All I could do was shake my head and enter the kitchen.

I wasn't aware of it, but while Shirley and I were talking, Georgie was focused on his mother's smoking. He was very bothered by his mother's choice to smoke, despite his unsuccessful attempts to discourage her...as well as her doctor's warnings. He had tried crying, yelling, pleading, and even *not* speaking to her. Sometimes it worked but, for a brief period of time. Most of the time, she would only wait until he left the house to sneak another cigarette.

Soon the commotion in the house caught my attention again, jarring me back to reality. I welcomed it. Somehow it drowned out the sadness haunting the house and my mind. Well, maybe it didn't, but it provided me with a temporary sense of relief. My mind needed the break.

After not finding anything else in the kitchen to rearrange or re-clean, I joined Shirley and the family again. I found a chair at the dining room table and blended in.

"Momma's hair was just as pretty and grey. They sure did a great job on Momma, didn't they?" Shirley didn't miss a beat. She picked up right where we left off.

"Ciavarelli is good. When it's my time to be laid to rest, I know I want Ciavarelli to take care of me. You hear me Georgie?"

She turned her head in the direction of her son as he reclined in Poppa's chair. This time, she didn't think that smoking would bother her son. She just thought that he would understand and, to some degree, even give her permission to smoke. This was not the case. He was fuming inside, to the point that he chose not to answer his mother.

"I said I want Ciavarelli to take care of my body when-"

"God, Mom, do you have to talk about that now?"

Shirley recognized that sound in her son's voice. She knew that she was about to be lectured and read the riot act. So, she adjusted in her seat and began looking through an Ebony magazine.

"I'm just saying. I know that you don't like for me to talk about my death, but we all know that we are born into this world, live and then-"

"Die! We die mom. I know...*we all know*. You keep telling me this over and over and over again. But you're alive. You are still alive, so please stop talking about death. Besides, how many times do I have to ask and plead before you stop smoking?"

"He's right Shirley. The boy has a point," I said.

In one swift movement, Shirley turned in my direction and glared at me. "Who asked you anyway? This is my last one. Besides, I just smoked this one today. It calms me."

George sat back in his chair, crossing his arms, as the family began to laugh at Shirley's ridiculous comment. They all knew that this was not the first, nor last cigarette she would ever have.

"This is your third or fourth one by my count. Go on and smoke all you want. Pretty soon we'll be really talking about death-*your* death," Georgie said, as he turned his back to his mother.

"Now you watch your mouth young man. I'm still your mother and before I let you think that you're going to speak to me any old kind of way, I'll-"

Before Shirley could finish her thought, Sarah had quietly opened the front door and moved unobtrusively through the house and into the kitchen. She didn't look at anyone. She didn't speak to anyone. Each and every movement was calculated. All she wanted to do was to avoid contact and communication with everyone. Each step she took created a sense of tension and awkwardness to all she passed.

Georgie was glad for this interruption, because he knew that his mother was going to continue with her dissertation on death, smoking, and Ciavarelli. Shirley, although not facing Georgie, had not forgotten the conversation.

"I'll..."

It was my turn to intervene and bring about a sense of peace.

"Shirley, help me in the kitchen."

Shirley knew I didn't need any help-especially help in the kitchen. Georgie relaxed into his seat. He knew that his mother would soon pick up where she left off. It may not be today or tomorrow, but she would finish what she had to say. He laughed to himself, as he was satisfied with his momentary win. His mom was a pro at this game and he knew from the beginning of the conversation that she would be the victor.

As Shirley and I rose from our seats, Sarah re-joined the family in the dining room. She remained quiet and continued to avoid eye contact, even with Shirley and me. It was almost as if she knew what I was about to do. She knew that I would be bringing Shirley into the kitchen to talk with her. She was two steps ahead. As uncomfortable as it was for her, she knew that the only way to escape our inquiries was to join the family.

As she carried plates, glasses, and table setting back and forth from the kitchen, we attempted to assist, but was met with a very short and curt reply, "I've got it."

Although I was slightly offended, I knew my sister. She didn't want to talk and definitely would not be forced to talk. If she had anything to say, she would do so on her own terms.

"I'll finish setting the table if you and Shirley check on dinner."

I couldn't help but feel a little saddened by Sarah's desperation. She would do anything to avoid discussing her feelings. I wanted to be supportive, but dinner needed to be served and Shirley and I would do just as she asked. After all, we were sisters and we loved each other.

It was almost like old times as the grandchildren, great-grandchildren, cousins, nephews, and nieces ran around the house playing, watching television, and paging through photo albums. Instead of a repast it seemed more like a family reunion. Bradie, Georgie, and Wendy sat in the living room retelling stories from the past; stories from a happier time. A time when family meant more than just summer vacations, backyard picnics, weddings, and soul train lines. I miss those days.

"Do y'all remember when we were little and Nana used to tell us to either stay in the house or outside? It don't make no sense running in and out let'in all those flies," Bradie said as he kicked off his shoes.

My Bradie was a sweet child that would do anything for anyone. He was naive to the cruelties of the world. I guess I am to blame for that. I only wanted to protect him. My intentions were never to smother him. A mother's duty is to guide and protect her children. Sometimes, I think I overprotected him and never allowed him to learn some of life's more harsh lessons on his own. He's strong and can think for himself. He will do more than just survive. He has a purpose.

"Oh wait. Don't forget when Nana would always call you by everyone else's name but your own," laughed George as he stood to imitate Momma.

"Wendy, Georgie, Skippy, Bradie...stop all that running around up there before someone gets hurt."

He was right. Momma had many strengths, but remembering your name wasn't one of them. I guess she earned being forgetful when she raised a family like ours. There were so many children hugging and kissing on her that I even found it difficult to remember everyone's name myself. Georgie was just like Shirley. He was well spoken, neat, and knew just how to say exactly what he meant. He never stumbled over his words.

"Remember Nana and her cute little crooked finger?" interjected Wendy.

"I sure remember. As many times as you all set me up to get in trouble. I tried telling Nana that it wasn't me doing whatever she thought I was going on, but it never failed. I would always be the one to get into trouble," added Bradie.

"Well, you never learned did you. We would set you up every time. Wait, do you all remember how Nana would never use the vacuum?" Wendy continued.

"Oh my God, I totally forgot about that old broom. Nana would start upstairs sweeping and make her way down the stairs with not a dust pan, but with a piece of bent up cardboard, to pick up the trash," recollected Georgie.

Wendy stood and began to mock Momma. It's funny how laughter makes the worst of situations appear better. It was almost as if things were back to normal, but once the laughter stopped, reality was right there to smack you dead in the face. It toyed with you...prolonging the inevitable, but until that dreaded moment came, the family continued to laugh.

The children were not the only ones who liked to have fun. I could tell by the expression on Shirley's face that she was up to something. She was a pro and was going to remind the younger, more inexperienced ones just why. As she made her way into the living room, Bradie, Georgie, and Wendy were unaware of what was about to happen to them. "Okay now," she interrupted. "you all may laugh at Nana, but when it came time to take care of you and cook for you all, she knew just what to do. At her age, she did well with just remembering who she was. You all should be fortunate to reach half her age."

"I know that's right Shirley," I chimed in.

"She damn sure knew what she was doing when it came time to taking care of you three. And if I remember, all of you at one point in time were fighting over who was going to spend the night with Momma and Daddy. She never said no and made room for everyone."

In that moment, Bradie, Georgie, and Wendy fell silent. They were ashamed of themselves. They didn't mean any harm. All they wanted to do was have some fun. They were only joking around. They looked so pitiful. I could hardly contain myself. I wanted to break out laughing, but they needed just a little more time to stew in their juices.

"How dare you talk about Momma," continued Shirley. "She was good to you three." Victory was close and she could feel it. Shirley walked back into the dining room and sat back in her chair. No one said a word. I'm sure some thought many things, but never uttered one syllable in the children's defense. As she sat in her chair, she struck one single match, lit another cigarette, inhaled and blew out a cloud of grey smoke.

"Do you all remember the day when Momma hit Daddy in the head so hard with Buzzy's red fire truck that she thought she had killed him?" Shirley said as she busted out laughing.

Soon the entire family roared with laughter. Not only were they laughing at Bradie, Georgie, and Wendy, they were laughing at the memory of Momma hitting Daddy in the head with the fire truck.

Finally, I could let it go. I couldn't contain myself as I recalled what Momma shouted that day. "Oh God...I killed him! I killed him! Get up Philip...please get up."

The family roared with hysteria except for the three cousins. They were mad. They were tricked by the queen of trickery. They would never live this moment down in their lives and knew that somewhere down the road, at some other family gathering, they would be the butt of someone's joke. As the family began to sigh, they continued their sharing of warm memories. The great-grandchildren sat and listened and realized that death had robbed them of their chance to create their own memories with Momma. As the family dispersed again throughout the house, attention was given to a small child playing alone by the living room couch. Pookie, the daughter of Momma's favorite grandchild, was the apple of Momma's eye. There is no way of describing how important this great-grandchild was to the survival of the family and especially Momma. She had given Momma the most important gift ever, the desire to live. When Pookie was born, Momma was slowly withering away. She grew old and tired and did not have the will to fight anymore. Although the family did their best to encourage her to be strong and not give up; nothing seemed to be working until that amazing day when Tee-Dee placed Pookie in the arms of Momma. Momma just beamed with joy. She bounced back and decided to live just a little bit longer. Pookie brought a smile to a wrinkled old face that had seen its best and worst of times. Momma was given another reason to live.

Pookie was loved by all. She just brought life back into the house and into the lives of many. Truth be told, she even saved me and my sisters. Yes, we loved each other, but our sisterly bond was tethered. Pookie gave us a reason to get together, to talk and to spend quality time with each other again. It sure was nice. I love my sisters.

Pookie especially brought a smile to Sarah's face. Sarah adored Pookie and did everything for her. There was nothing that was too good for Pookie. If it made her happy, Pookie got it. As Pookie ran around the house, dodging table corners, shoes left in the middle of the floor, and sharp objects, Sarah never took her eyes off her. Little did we know that Pookie was at it again. She was saving the life of yet another loved one. As Pookie rounded the corner in the dining room, without warning, she tripped over a bag that had been carelessly placed in the middle of the floor. She was falling and falling in the direction of the corner of an end table; until two brown arms reached down and saved her from mishap. Sarah was there and before Pookie could scream, she was rocked back and forth in her arms.

"Now see there...just stop all that running around before you fall again and scar those pretty little knees of yours," chastised Sarah.

All we could do was stop and savor the moment. It was like hearing Momma's precious voice all over again. I fought back the tears welling up in my eyes and knew that Shirley was watching me. I couldn't look at her. All I could do was silently call out, "Momma."

Pookie was so innocent and unaware of her importance. Like any other child whose sole purpose in life was to play, she hopped down from Sarah's lap and pulled her in the direction of Momma's room.

"Sarie, let's go upstairs and play." Sarah smiled at her ball of sunshine.

"Wait a minute Poo...just wait sweetheart. You better slow down before we both fall." As Sarah and Pookie climb the stairs leading to Momma's room, Shirley and I followed their every step until they rested on the top landing. We laughed to ourselves as we knew what was about to happen. In one swift movement, Pookies' two little feet were hoisted up into Sarah's arms and carried the rest of the way. We often joked with Sarah about never letting Pookie walk. Every time we turned around, Sarah was carrying Pooike. We would laugh and say, "Sarah, if you don't put the child down, she will never learn to walk." Although we knew that we were only joking, I think Sarah was slightly offended by our laughter and thought that we were judging her. Funny, the more things change, the more things stay the same. We still have to be careful of what we say to Sarah and how we say it. Sometimes I just don't know if she really knows how much we love her. Shirley shifted in her chair, as she pulled one last time on the cigarette and then smashed it into the ashtray. She smiled to herself as she gazed out the window.

"If Sarah doesn't look and act like Momma, I don't know what." I looked at Shirley's profile and was struck with the awareness of how much she looked and acted like Daddy. It frightened me; the way she tilted her head; the way she sat in the chair; even the way she held her cigarette, except Daddy would be smoking a cigar. It was as if he was sitting in his favorite chair waiting on Momma to set the table and serve dinner.

"She's Momma up and down," I agreed.

"All right," interrupted Laura, my first cousin. "It's time to eat."

"Come on, the food is ready," shouted June, Laura's sister.

We were grateful for family, especially Laura and June. They were more like sisters to us. We all grew up together and shared so many wonderful memories. They were always there behind the scenes helping out never complaining or asking for anything in return. That's what family is all about; being there for each other through the good times and bad.

*   *   *   *

As the family moved towards the dining room table, Sarah and Pookie entered my room, Momma's room, and closed the door shutting out the rest of the world so as to not intrude on their private moment. Sarah hesitated before entering the room. She was overwhelmed by a sudden rush of awareness. Her memories were fresh and all too real. The last time she had been in this room was during the time that Momma laid motionless on the bed awaiting death. It's funny how our memories can play tricks on us. Sarah could smell the cancer in the room. She could hear Momma panting trying to catch her breath. Each breath drew her closer and closer to death. Without warning, Sarah was forcefully pulled back into reality by Pookie's gentle tug on her dress. "Sarie come on. Let's play." Sarah closed her eyes and took a deep breath.

"Come on girl, get it together," She said as she shook herself. Downstairs, the family was unaware of Sarah's struggle. By this time, they had gathered around the table awaiting the blessing of the food. "Come on Brad and bless the food," requested Shirley. "And please make it short. You know how I like my food H.O.T, hot. I can't stand no cold food." As the family laughed, they gathered tightly nestled around the table holding hands. Their strength would help them endure their recent tragedy and loss and prepare them for future sorrows. "Family is important. Family means the world to me, it gives me purpose and the will to continue living. Brad smiled as he firmly grasped the hands of his cousins Wendy and Georgie.

"Okay, Aunt Shirley. Let us all bow our heads in prayer.

Dear Heavenly Father, we are so thankful for the
food that has been prepared for the nourishment of
our bodies. We ask you to bless the hands that have
prepared the food dear Father and watch over them."

Brad began to feel something welling up on the inside of his body. The feeling was indescribable yet familiar. He enjoyed praying. It made him feel peaceful and reassured him that everything was going to be alright.

Heavenly Father, we are so thankful for each and
every family member that is assembled here today
to share in the home going services of our loved one,
affectionately called Nana. We bless you right now

Lord for we know that tomorrow is not promised.

The family supported Brad's prayer of Thanksgiving with moans and affirming shouts of praise, as they continued to bow their heads and sway back and forth.

"It is truly a pleasure to see yet another glorious day. Oh Father..."

All I could do was watch and wait. Shirley knew that her warning of keeping the prayer short had been lost among the shouts and screams of amens. She leaned forward and politely but deliberately cleared her throat. This was no ordinary clearing of her throat. This was an, *I done told you I like my food hot* clearing of her throat and *you are praying to damn long, now hurry up and finish* kind of cough. Brad heeded the warning ending his prayer quickly and returned to his seat without establishing any eye contact with his aunt. He knew she was looking directly at him and sure enough...she was

"In your most precious name we pray. Amen."

"Amen" echoed the family as they laughed hysterically. Soon the dining room was filled with sounds of silverware clanging, chairs squeaking, ice swishing around in glasses, and belts popping from too much good eating.

During all this commotion, Sarah and Pookie had remained in Momma's room. It was perfectly preserved just as she left it. Nothing was out of place. Her scent continued to linger in the air. Sarah took it all in. Then without warning, she glanced over and focused on a dimly lit corner in the room. There she found an old friend. It was the rocking chair that Momma once sat in. She smiled. No matter how hard she prayed to God to grant her one last favor, one last wish, she knew Momma wasn't coming back.

"Oh God, please just bring her back to me. I need to hear her voice one more time. I need you Momma."

As Sarah cried, she rested her weary frame in the chair. She found comfort in its curves as it seemed liked Momma was holding her in her arms one last time.

"Here Sarie, These are for you."

Sarah had almost forgotten that the small child was in the room with her. Pookie had placed three small blocks in the center of her lap. Sarah smiled as she peered into the eyes of the innocent child.

"Thank you, sweetheart."

As Sarah held one of the blocks in the palm of her hand, she was unaware of the song Pookie was singing.

> *"We love you, Pookie. Oh yes we do. We love you,*
> *Pookie, oh yes it's true. When you're not with us*
> *we're blue. Oh, Pookie, we love you."*

It was the *Pookie Song* that Shirley had sung on many occasions when we were attempting to bathe Pookie and put her down for her afternoon nap. Sarah and I were no singers by any means, but we adored Pookie and knew that the only chance we stood at getting this child to sleep was to sing our crude version of the *Pookie Song*. It usually took about four to five rounds of singing before we could get Pookie to fall asleep.

> *"We love you Pookie oh yes we do. We love you*
> *Pookie oh yes it's true. When you're not with us we're*
> *blue. Oh Pookie we love you."*

Pookie was insightful for a child her age. She knew that something was wrong with Sarah. As she looked up at Sarah, she noticed a tear streaking down her cheek. Pookie slowly stood to her feet and moved closer and closer to Sarah. She rested one small finger on her cheek stopping the tear from flowing any further. "Sarie... don't cry. Come on...play."

Sarah placed her hand over Pookie's finger and pressed it gently into her face then slowly over her lips. She loved Pookie as her own and would do anything for her.

"I'm sorry sweetheart. Here let's play build a block."

Pookie laughed as she recognized the familiar smile on Sarah's face.

"I love you Sarie."

"And I love you my dear, sweet Pookie Poo."

As Sarah leaned forward to kiss Pookie on her forehead, the block placed in her lap fell to the floor and rolled under the bed.

"Oh dear."

"Here Sarie, I'll get it"

"No honey, you might bump your head. Let me get it."

The last thing that Sarah wanted was for Pookie to hurt herself while she was in her care. She would never forgive herself if the unthinkable happened. She remembered the time that Momma was holding Pookie and her eyeglass frame mistakenly scratched Pookie's eye and we had to rush her to the hospital. She never forgave herself and made sure to take off her glasses every time there after when she held her.

Sarah eased her way from the chair to the floor reaching for the block.

"I don't see it, Poo."

Sarah reached further under the bed and finally felt the block. As she began to pull the block towards her, her hand brushed up against another unfamiliar object.

"What's this?'

Sarah quickly pulled the block out from under the bed and placed it in the hands of Pookie. "Here honey. Here's your block. Now go on and play. Sarie will be right there to help you build the biggest, tallest skyscraper there ever was."

Pookie did just as she was told. Sarah smiled to herself as she attempted to look under the bed to find the unfamiliar object that brushed up against her hand. She was unable to clearly see what was under the bed as the room was dimly lit. As she desperately reached as far as she could, she became aware of how fast and irregular her heart was beating. As her level of frustration built, she took one last, deep breath, and stretched as far as she could under the bed.

"Oh my God," Sarah silently whispered to herself. "It can't be."

With the object firmly grasped in her hand, Sarah slowly made her way back to the rocking chair and stared at her clenched fist. She was reluctant to open her hand, as she feared the unknown. As her fingertips gently traced its edges, Sarah gazed outside the window.

"It can't be. It just can't be."

Tears streamed down Sarah's face as she opened her hand.

"Oh Momma."

There in the middle of Sarah's palm was Momma's eyeglasses. We had searched all over the house for Momma's glasses on the day she died, but could not find them. As Pookie continued to play innocently with her blocks, she slowly glanced up at Sarah and noticed Sarah crying.

"Sarie, what's wrong? Don't cry, Sarie. Please don't cry."

Pookie placed her hand on Sarah's soft, moist cheek and stared confusingly into Sarah's eyes. How could such a young child be so in tune with the worries of those around her? As Sarah became aware of Pookie's gentle touch, she peered into the eyes of the innocent young child and smiled, "Oh baby, honey, Sarah's fine. I just love you so much."

"Why are you crying?" Pookie asked as she climbed into Sarah's lap. "I miss her too, Sarie."

A surge of emotions flooded Sarah's heart as she wrapped Pookie in her arms and she began singing, "I love you Pookie, oh yes I do. I love you Pookie oh yes it's true..." As Sarah continued to rock Pookie back and forth in her arms, she found it more and more difficult to utter another word.

"When you're...when you're...not..."

Pookie slowly raised her head from resting on Sarah's breast and quietly sang, "When you're not with us, we're blue. Oh Pookie we love you."

"Oh, Poo Bear..."

Sarah was speechless. All she could do was thank God for the sweet little girl resting in her arms. As Sarah and Pookie continued to share in a precious tender moment, Wendy, who had been assisting me and Shirley with serving the food, became aware that her mother had been absent from the family gathering for a while now. She was concerned and could sense that something was wrong.

"Aunt Shirley, I'll be right back to help finish serving. I need to go and check on my mom."

"Go on ahead sweetheart...tell them that their food is getting cold and I'm not gonna be on my feet all day serving. My legs are killing me right now and I need to get off of them. Once I sit down, I'm not thinking about getting back up for nobody."

"Yes ma'am."

Wendy, with her youthfulness, ran up the stars with ease.

"Lord, would you look at that," I said as I watched Wendy climb the stairs with no problem. "There used to be a time when I could do-"

"Sissy please...don't do it to yourself honey. Yes, there used to be a time, but that time sure as hell ain't here no more," Shirley said as she plopped down in the nearest chair.

"Now I'm down ya'll and don't ask me to do nothing else. I done served you and I ain't serving no more."

As Wendy neared the bedroom she could hear the faint sound of singing coming from the room. She smiled to herself as she was familiar with the song being sung. "*I love you Pookie, oh yes I do. I love you...*" Wendy sang as she opened the bedroom door. "Mom-"

Wendy was startled as she locked eyes on her mother holding Pookie in the dimly lit room. "Mom...Pookie, honey, come on with me."

Sarah unwrapped her arms and helped Pookie out of her lap. She couldn't look at her daughter. Wendy knew her mother. She couldn't hide anything from Wendy. She knew that although Wendy would not confront her mother about what was happening, she was fully aware that it would only be a short time before Wendy would reach Shirley and me to tell us what was going on.

"Bye Sarie," Pookie waved as she left the room with Wendy.

As Wendy neared the last step, Shirley noticed the bewildered look on Wendy's face.

"Honey, what's wrong?"

"I'm not sure, but my mother is upstairs crying."

"Don't worry, I'll get Gert and we'll go see what's the matter." Shirley called for me to come over to her.

"Gert, Wendy said Sarah's upstairs not doing too well. I think we need to check on her." As Shirley and I climbed the stairs, we reached the top step and paused to catch our breath and then entered the room.

"Sarah, what's wrong honey?" Shirley asked as she sat on the corner of the bed. I knew what Sarah was going through. Shirley was stronger than Sarah and me concerning dealing with our emotions. She was a rock, someone you could count on to help you through trying situations. I was the overemotional one. I was sensitive to the pain of others and sometimes knew that a good cry was needed to help you through the day. "Sarah...oh honey, we're here," I said.

I stood behind Sarah and gently rested her head on my hip.

"Let it go Sarah. Go ahead, just let it go. She's in a better place now sweetheart. No more suffering. No more pain. No more sickness." As Shirley ran her hand back and forth over the embroidered, white blanket on the bed, she realized that this was the first time that she had been back in Momma's room since that fateful night.

"I miss you, Momma. You're in a better place sweetheart."

It wasn't until Shirley mentioned Momma that I realized what Sarah was holding in the fold of her hand.

"Yes...yes she is. I'm gonna miss her."

"Calm yourself, Gertrude before you get yourself all upset," Shirley said.

"Lord knows I'm gonna miss her!" I shouted

"We're all going to miss her. She fought a good fight and died the way she always dreamed of; with her family surrounding her. She wasn't even supposed to live this long, remember? The doctor had given her only a couple of months and here she lived for another three years."

"You're right, Shirley. I know."

"And God knows if it wasn't for Pookie, she would have given up long ago."

"I know, Shirley. I know. She sure did bring Momma back to us." In one quick jerking movement, Sarah stood to her feet and attempted to run out the room. I couldn't grab her fast enough. I knew Sarah. She wanted to run away from the pain inside and to not have to deal with the obvious. Hell, I wanted to run too.

"Sarah, don't!"

Shirley was quick on her feet and was able to grab Sarah before she reached the bedroom door. "Sarah-"

"I hate God for taking my Momma. I hate Him!" Sarah screamed.

"I know, Sarah. I know."

"No Shirley, you don't. I need Momma. I need her to be here

and..."

"And what Sarah?" I asked.

"I just need her! I want her back. I want her back Shirley!"

The room fell silent as Shirley led Sarah back to the chair she was sitting in and to my outstretched arms.

"She was my *best friend*." Sarah wept in my arms.

"How many more have to die? How many more have to die? It's just not fair!" I mumbled to myself.

The only thing that I could do was just embrace my dear sister. I just held her tightly in my arms and cried with her. "It's just not fair! Why...it's just not fair!" Shirley rose from the bed and walked over to Sarah and me.

"Shirley make it better. Please make it better," I pleaded. "They keep dying! How many more have to die? They're gone Shirley! Momma's gone! Ida, Mabel, Warnie, Barkley, Mae Mae...my Fred...too many! I can't take it anymore!"

"Gertrude calm yourself before you get all worked up and make yourself sick."

"I'm afraid!" Sarah cried over and over again.

"Sarah-"

"I'm so afraid!" Sarah interrupted.

"How many more have to die from...oh, God!" Sarah shrieked. "I can't say it!" "How many more have to die from-"

"Shirley, don't! Please, don't say it," I interrupted.

"No, Gert. We walk around here on *eggshells,* afraid of thinking about *it*...afraid of talking about *it*...afraid of getting *it*."

"Shirley, please don't," I begged. Sarah just buried her head deeper and deeper in my chest. "Enough! Enough of this! How many more have to die from cancer?"

I couldn't breathe. I couldn't move. What had Shirley done?

"How many more have to die from cancer?" Shirley continued. "There, it's been said. But, I tell you this, I'll be damned if I am going to walk around this house anymore afraid of facing *it*. We'll be fine. Do you hear me? We will be fine!"

"Oh Shirley. Shirley I-" I sobbed.

"Gert, enough. We will be fine. Now, pull yourself together. We have each other and we will get through this. We've been through worse than this before and made it. We will all be just fine." Shirley said as she placed her hand on Sarah's head.

"Do you hear me Sarah? I know you're scared, but we will be just fine."

"Fine." Sarah repeated

"Fine," Shirley reassured her. "Now let's get back downstairs and eat some of my pound cake. You know that always makes things better."

"Girl, you sure are right," I laughed.

Shirley, Sarah and I embraced one last time. As Shirley and I left the room, Sarah fell back and placed the eye glasses in the center of the bed and walked to the door.

"Fine...I hope so."

CHAPTER THREE

Not Me Lord

Time waits for no one. It just fools you into believing that it heals all wounds; but does it? Hell no! *Hell no,* I say.

I think people just say this because it's the only thing that they have to hold on to. It's the only thing that keeps hope alive. I'm done hoping and believing in those sayings from the past. For all I care, they can go straight to hell. I buried my heart in the ground the day that I had to bury Momma six feet under. What good does it do you to hold onto hope anyway? I don't know what to believe anymore. I just miss my Momma.

It hurts like hell inside and it just won't go away. The throbbing is killing me. The aching is unbearable. Some days, I just lie in the bed and don't even have the will to go on, but I know Momma wouldn't want that for me or for anyone. What would have happened if she just gave up and didn't fight? Was it even worth fighting for? Was her fighting in vain? I mean when you really look at it, death won anyway.

Well, I don't know the answer and don't know if I'll ever know the answer, but Momma sure died with her dignity. She held onto her faith and never turned her back on the Lord. I wonder if I'll be the same when my time comes or will I try bargaining with death or beg for my life? Who knows? I guess

I'll just have to wait until death comes a knocking on my door.

No one really got over Momma's death. We all just learned how to live life without her. The thought of living without Momma was difficult to grasp. Death can wreak havoc on a family. It can tear a family apart, or it can bring a family closer.

Thankfully, it brought our family closer. It strengthened the existing bond between some and brought others back to familiar ground. We would need that strong family bond to get through the coming times ahead of us. Our faith in God and each other would soon be tested.

I wonder if death sometimes feels sorry for you. I laugh at myself when I think of such a thought. Sometimes it feels like death just knows that what it is about to deliver is not even fair. Death's gift sometimes is just a break from all the pain. Although the break is temporary, it is appreciated. Thanks, death.

When Bradie and I moved back home, we couldn't bear the thought of changing anything around. We left it just like Momma had it. The furniture, color of the drapes, and even the place settings were just as she had left them. I made the middle room my room and Bradie reluctantly took the front room - Momma's room.

No one wanted to sleep in the back room. There was something about that back room that scared the hell out of us all. I refused to allow death to run me out of my own house; this house that I grew up in and loved so dearly.

I know Bradie. He's the scary type and would often call out in the middle of the night, "Mom, you okay?"

I knew that he was only calling out for me to say in return, "Yes honey," and then ask, "you?"

It tickled me something, but I understood. My little man was trying to be the man of the house and watch over me. I guess secretly, I did more watching over him.

I continued to work at Ambler Rest Center, a nursing home for the elderly. I had a high school education and was proud of my work. Even though I was a Nurse's Assistant, I knew I was just as important as those damn nurses who would look down their noses at me because the patients would *always ask for Gert*. Don't get me wrong, I had my days with some of those patients who thought we were *back in the day*.

"Come here girly," some old white, racist bag would call out to me.

"Girl don't you hear me calling you?" they would say, as if I was supposed to stop everything and jump to their call and say, "No ma'am, I didn't hear you."

The hell, I tell you. I wish the hell one of those old bags would even think to fix their mouths to say some foolishness like that out loud. They'd sit in their shit all day.

I'd tell them, "Wipe your own ass if that's how you gonna talk to me."

I watched what I said (some of the time), but honey, there were times I just had to put them in their place. I didn't care if it cost me my job. The Lord always made a way out of no way. Sometimes I did bite my tongue. I had to think about Bradie and putting him through school. Lord knows I don't know how I'm gonna do it, but I sure as hell am. I did it for Skippy and I'm gonna do it for Bradie. If I had to wipe all the asses in the nursing home and take all the shit they gave me, I would do it for my children. Any mother would do the same without hesitating. Your kids always come first.

My oldest son, Skippy, was tough and had common sense. He lived in Atlanta, Georgia and knew how to take care of himself. Hell, he's just like me. Ain't no one gonna walk over me and he sure was the spitting image of his Dear old mother.

I'm proud of Skippy. I know I don't tell him this enough, but I sure am proud of him. He made something of himself.

Bradie on the other hand, well, I think I over protected him. Fred used to always say, "Let the boy be a boy. You ain't always gonna be around to fight his battles. Let'm grow the hell up." He was right, but I just felt the need to always watch over him. Bradie didn't have the common sense that Skippy had. He was too trusting and saw the good in everyone even when there was no good to be seen. He was smart and was heading to college; Morehouse College. I sure didn't want him to go that far away from me and tried my best to stop him. I called myself, telling Daddy that he needed to tell Bradie that he couldn't go, but Shirley told me I was dead wrong. Skippy and Marsha lived in Georgia and would look after him. Somehow that made me feel a little bit better...not much, but some.

*   *   *   *

"I'll see ya later Gert,"Alice, one of my few and only friends, called as she slammed her time card on the table. "The more I seem to work, the less money I seem to make." It was time to leave this old hell hole for the day. I had a long walk ahead of me and it was hot as could be out there.

The walk home would help clear my mind of all that stuff from work. I often thought about Momma and at times, still find myself rushing home to take care of her. On many a day, I had to stop myself from damn near running to get home. I had to slow my thoughts down and remind myself that Momma was gone. This was one of those days.

It was like a routine. I clocked out, grabbed my bag, and hit the pavement.

This day was no different from any other day. I had Momma on my mind. My thoughts were racing and my heart was pounding. I couldn't catch my breath and just needed to stop for a second, but I didn't. I just kept on walking.

I wasn't paying attention to anything. If I had only looked up;

if I had only looked up, I would have seen that damn pothole. Before I knew it, I went right down. I fell flat on my face. The pain was something bad. It jarred me so that I couldn't even get myself up off the ground. If it wasn't for this kind, old man driving by, I don't know what I would have done.

"You okay, miss?" he yelled, as he helped me to my feet.

"Oh Lord. Thank You, Sir. I don't know what is wrong with me! I just have so much on my mind and...well, I'll be fine."

The man appeared reluctant to leave my side.

"Are you sure you're fine? I could-"

"No sir, that won't be necessary. I'll be just fine. I only live right around the corner from here. Please, don't worry."

The man shrugged his shoulders, got back into his car and drove off.

Funny, if you don't slow yourself down, God sure will.

I attempted to walk in the direction of my home, but stammered to a halt. I felt this excruciating pain throbbing in the middle of my chest. The more I breathed, the more it throbbed. It damn near knocked me flat off my feet again. I never even took the time to see if I had hurt myself.

I was rushing home only out of habit. There was no Momma to take care of. There was no laundry to fold, no clothes to be washed, no medicine to give, there was nothing but emptiness. I had no Momma to take care of.

"Damn!" I shouted as the pain worsened. I just happened to look down and noticed that my hands were covered in blood.

"What in the name of God is this?" Not only were my hands bleeding, but I noticed that my blouse was covered in blood as well.

"Jesus! Oh Lord what...," I began to shake my head in an attempt to block out all the worries that filled my mind. The more I tried to get my thoughts together, the more my thoughts seemed to race.

Gert, honey...now you just calm yourself. Get yourself together, right now! The blood frightened me. My blouse was saturated.

I needed to get home. I prayed to God to give me the strength just to make it home. Usually, on any given day I would have been stopped by someone who lived in my community and offered a ride home. No one came by today.

"Lord, please help me get home," I cried out to the Heavens above. "Please, just get me home God."

The walk home seemed to take forever. With each step I took, the more the pain surged from my chest.

"God!" The pain was overwhelming.

"Just a little bit further Gert. Just a little bit further," I kept repeating to myself.

Soon, I saw the church on the corner. Bethlehem Baptist Church. I was never happier to see those red, double doors in my life. I just had to make it up Trewellyn Avenue.

Honey, you're almost home. Just a little further Gert. Just a little further.

At last I was home. "11070 Trewellyn Avenue," I read the numbers on the mailbox.

As I leaned against the wood-framed door to the house, I barely was able to get the key in the door. All I could think about was resting my nerves. I just wanted to get off my feet and rest my nerves. As the door flung open, I screamed,

"Brad, oh my God. Bradie!" Before I knew it, I fell into the arm of my baby. "Mom? Mom! What happened? What happened to you?"

I couldn't catch my breath as the pain by this time was overwhelming. "Honey, please...please just get me to the couch. Mommy will be alright. Just get me to the couch."

Bradie, God bless him. He was a sweet child. I knew that he was scared for me and needed to hear that I was fine, but the truth of the matter is I wasn't. I was scared myself.

"But mom...mom-"

"Bradie, just get me to the couch!" I didn't mean to yell at him, but I couldn't take it anymore. I had to sit down to get myself together.

"Okay mom, I'm sorry. You're just scaring me, that's all." As he gently rested me on the couch, I sighed in an attempt to manage the pain, but it was useless. I couldn't let on to Bradie that I was scared. I did what any mother would have done in a case like this, I lied.

"Your hand! Mom, your hand is bleeding!"

"Honey, I'm fine. Please don't worry about Mommy."

"No mom, you're not fine...you're *not*. I'm gonna call Aunt Shirley."

"I *said* I'm fine!"

Bradie stopped dead in his tracks. I could see the look of fear in his eyes.

"Baby, I'm sorry, baby. Mommy didn't mean to yell. Look, I just need to lay down for a little bit. I just fell, that's all. Now please just help me to my room. I'm gonna be just fine sweetheart."

Despite hearing what I said, Bradie knew me. He knew that regardless of how much pain I was in, I would never tell him the truth.

"Mom, you are always trying to protect me. You are always trying to shield me from the truth. I can handle it, Mommy. If you need me, I'm here." All I could do was look at my child. He was all grown up and was ready to become a man. All he ever wanted from me was to be loved. He didn't care about anything else in the world. He just wanted his mother's love.

"My sweet Bradie. Oh, my sweet child..." No matter how much it killed me inside to not tell him the truth, I had to lie. He was about to graduate and didn't need to have anything else but living on his mind. I was gonna be alright. There was no other option in my mind. I was gonna be just fine.

"Baby, just take Mommy to her bedroom. Rest your mind and know that I am fine honey." Bradie gently took hold of both my hands. At first he just stared longingly at the cuts and dried blood covering my palms. Slowly he lifted his eyes until he fixed his gaze on my worn brow. "Bradie, what is it?"

He never said a word. All he did was lean in and kiss my forehead.

"Honey...what-"

"You wouldn't lie to me, would you?"

"Oh Bradie. Why would you say such a thing?" He said it because he knew it was true. He looked into my eyes as if he knew there was something wrong and I wasn't telling him.

"Here," I called out as I tried to stand to my feet. "Baby, don't worry about your old mother. Like I said, I'll be just fine. Now help me to my bedroom."

As Bradie grasped me under my arm, I knew something was wrong. I felt something deep down at the core of my soul. Something was wrong. I just couldn't show it in front of him. As we climbed the stairs leading to the bedroom, I grimaced in pain. It was so bad that I had to turn my head away to hide the frown on my face.

"Mom, you o.k.?"

"Yes, honey. It's just the stairs that tire me out."

Brad led me directly to my bedroom door. "I can take it from here."

"Mom..."

"Now just listen to me. Mommy's got it from here. Now, you go on downstairs and let me get myself together."

"But Mom..."

"Honey, please just do as I say. I'll call you if I need you. Besides, Shirley will be up in just a few. You know she always stops by after work to have her-"

"Last cigarette," Brad said as we both laughed knowing Shirley has been saying her last cigarette for as long as we both could remember. "You promise to call me if you need me?"

"I said I would. Now go on."

As Bradie left my side and headed back downstairs, I fell into the door. "Jesus," I called out in pain. Slowly I turned the knob and walked into the room. I found comfort in my room, as it was my place of solace. It was in this very room, I could talk to God and find peace. No one knew what it was like to be me. I was always seen as the tough one. I was the fighter in the family. I cursed when I needed to, put you in your place and out the house if I had to.

But there was another side to me that I never let others see. Things scared me. Uncertainty paralyzed me. God only knows how many times I called on Him to ease my mind. I wasn't this tough, unaffected woman who didn't have feelings. Inside I was a little girl wanting her mother. I did what I had to do because it was expected and necessary. If I didn't do it, who would?

*   *   *   *

As I sat on the corner of my bed, I stared at myself in the mirror. I was old. Who was this woman staring back at me? I didn't recognize her.

The blood and the blood-stained blouse I was wearing caught my attention. "What in God's name is this?"

As I slowly unbuttoned my blouse, I knew something was very wrong. It hurt just to move. With each button I managed to undo, I flinched in pain. Once they were all undone, I noticed a black and blue area over my left breast.

"Oh God...Jesus...what in the world?" I placed my hand over

the area and was immediately gripped by fear.

"A knot!" I covered my mouth, so as not to alarm Bradie.

"No, God, not a knot." I quickly dropped my hand to my side and closed my eyes. Maybe it wasn't a knot. Maybe I had gotten myself all upset and...let me calm down and look again. I didn't want to touch it again. I didn't want to feel the knot again. "Gert get a hold of yourself. You're overreacting." I took one deep breath and raised my hand to my chest.

"God! No, God!"

My scream was loud. It was so loud that it caught the attention of Bradie. "Mom!" I could hear Bradie running up the stairs. He was probably panicking. All I could do was jump up from the bed and lock the door. He couldn't enter the room. It would only frighten him.

"Mom? Mom, open the door. I can't get in. Open the door!" I knew I was wrong for locking him out. "Bradie, I'm sorry baby. Mommy's fine. Please go downstairs." Bradie wasn't buying my plea. He began banging on the door harder. "Mom, let me in! Let me in! I can't get in." I leaned with my back pressed up against the door, as tears ran down my face. "Bradie, go back downstairs. Mommy is fine."

"If you're fine then open up the door. I need to see that you're fine." I knew if I didn't do something quickly he was going to try his best to break down the door. "Honey..."

"Mom-"

"Okay, I'm opening the door." Slowly I cracked the door enough to show Bradie my face. "Mommy's fine honey. See I told you."

"Mom, what is going on?"

"I just tried taking off my blouse and, well, I'm just sore from the fall, that's all. You know I'm old," I said with a forced laugh. "I'm old and these bones don't move like they used to."

"Mom, let me in."

"Mommy's not dressed all the way. Let me put some clothes on and I'll call you when I'm done. Besides, I think I hear Shirley pulling up."

"Mom-"

"Go on and see if that's her. I'll be down in a minute."

"Mom."

"Go!"

"Fine, but I'll be back to check on you." As Bradie ran down the stairs again, I shut the door and exhaled. "Please let that be Shirley." As soon as Bradie hit the last step, the front door opened.

"Gertrude! Gertrude, come on down. Do I have something to tell you!"

"Hey, Aunt Shirley, Mom is upstairs and-" I knew my son. He was going to tell Shirley all about what just happened. I mustered up enough strength to open the door and call out, "I'll be right down Shirley. Sissy, I hope whatever it is you have to tell me is good. Because after the day I had, I need some good old dirt."

Bradie tried his best to tell Shirley, but I couldn't let him. He didn't have to worry about me and besides, I'm not sure what was happening. "Aunt Shirley I need to-"

"Bradie, Honey, I think that's Georgie outside blowing for you. Don't you have somewhere to go?"

"Oh, I almost forgot. Georgie wants me to take a ride with him to the airport." Shirley, by this time, had wandered over to the couch and sat down. She was trying to wait for Bradie to leave so she could strike up a cigarette.

"Honey, I'm sorry. I forgot to tell you. Georgie said come on, because he is running late. I got so into thinking about that gossip I had to tell your mother, I plum forgot."

Soon Bradie's last attempt to tell Shirley what was going on was interrupted by the sound of a car horn. It was Georgie, and from the sound of his blowing, he was ready to go. "I'm coming," Bradie yelled out the front door. "I'll be right there." From a distance you could hear Georgie yelling back, "Look, if you're not out here in two minutes, I'm gonna-"

"I said I'm coming. Don't start with me Georgie."

Shirley couldn't wait any longer. She needed to light up and take a long drag from the cigarette. "Honey, please just go on with that son of mine. If he blows on that horn one more time, I'm gonna scream."

"Okay, Aunt Shirley. I'm going, but there's something I need-" With my last ounce of strength, I yelled from the top of the stairs, "Bradie, didn't Shirley tell you to go on? Now, get on before Georgie blows that horn one more time!"

"Fine," Bradie said as he slammed the front door. As soon as I heard the door slam, I slumped over in pain.

"Shirley!" I screamed from the top of the steps. "Shirley, I need you. Help me!"

Shirley jumped to her feet and ran as fast as her legs would allow her up the stairs. "Gert? Sissy, what's the matter?" As she reached the top step, the pain was so intense that I couldn't even speak.

"Gertrude! Gertrude what in God's name?"

All I could do was gesture for her to take me back into the bedroom and sit me in the chair. "Gertrude? Gert, you're scaring me. What is going on?"

I raised my hand in an attempt to ease Shirley's worries, but it was no good.

"Gert, I'm gonna call the ambulance. We have to get you-"

"No! Oh, Shirley, on my way home from work, I was walking and not paying attention, and before I knew it I went right down."

"You fell?" Shirley asked as she took a seat on the corner of the bed.

"Yes, Sissy. I fell right on my hands. See?"

I placed one hand in Shirley's lap. I never let go of my blouse with the other. My fingers were so tightly clenched around the blouse they started cramping. I had to keep my blouse closed. I didn't want Shirley to see the bruised area above my breast. "Sissy, it's all cut up. Oh, honey, you must have hurt yourself something bad. Here, let me see the other hand." Shirley attempted to pry my hand loose, but I wouldn't let her. "Shirley, I'm fine."

"No, Gert. Let me see your other hand. You're hurt. I need to see." She pulled my wrist with all her might, but I wouldn't let go. I was afraid of what she would say when she saw my chest.

"No, Sissy, I'm fine." Shirley wouldn't let go. She pulled and pulled and pulled. I couldn't take it anymore. I wanted to pass out. The pain was pulsating with such force, that with each pull, it knocked the breath clear out of me. "No, Shirley! No!"

"Gertrude Cox you let me see!" With one forceful gesture, I threw my hand up in the air and screamed, "I found a knot!"

Shirley didn't move. Soon the pain was replaced with a deep sense of fear. As the tears streamed down my face, I fell into Shirley's arms.

"What are you talking about a knot?"

"I found a knot on my chest; my breast Shirley, my breast."

"What did you say?"

"I found a knot on my breast."

As Shirley sat me back up in the chair, she cautiously opened my blouse. "Oh Gert. What in God's name?"

"Shirley, it's...a knot. Do you think that it could be-"

"Stop! Right now...you don't know what it is. It could be anything."

"It's...what if it is, cancer? I can't go anywhere yet. Skippy is on his feet, but Bradie...Bradie is about to graduate and go to college. He needs me. He's not ready to be without me. I need to be here for my children. I'm not ready!"

"Stop it, damn it! You're still alive and you'll stay that way. Now get yourself together. Do you hear me?"

Shirley was not one to become easily upset. She was the rock in our family. She remained in control of her emotions and would be the first to tell you that she just doesn't get upset like others. Sure she cries, but it's not one of those uncontrollable sobs. She will shed a few tears and that's it. I admire her. I'm just the total opposite. I scream, shout, yell and think of the worst case scenario first. "You're fine Sissy and will stay that way."

"O.k. Shirley."

"Now, I think that we should call Dr. Cruz and see if he is able to see you this evening. If not, I think that we should take you to the hospital." Just the mere mention of having to go to a hospital unnerved me. "I'm not going to no hospital! Once you go in, you never come out."

"Gert stop with all that foolish, old folks talking. You know damn well that's not the truth." "Shirley...I don't care what you say. If Dr. Cruz can't see me, I'm staying right here. No hospital!"

"Fine"

"Fine!"

"You sure know how to get the hell on my nerves," Shirley told me as she stood up from the bed. "Well...you sure know how to work my last nerve."

"Listen here Gert, I'm not the one who fell. I don't have to be-"

"I'm scared Shirley. Scared..."

I couldn't take it anymore. No matter what I told myself, all I could do was think about cancer. Momma just died from it and our family surely is stricken with it. There is no way around the fact that cancer is a part of our family...a living, breathing part of our family.

Shirley could tell that something was wrong with me. She normally would have cursed me out and then just went on about her way. This time, she just stood there motionless with her back to me "Shirley, I'm scared. I don't know what to do if it's-"

"Do you have Dr. Cruz's number?"

"Yes...it's in the back room by the lamp."

"I'll get it." Shirley left out the room and went into the back room. "Where did you say you put it?" "On the nightstand by the lamp...you see it?"

"Hold on..."

"Shirley, do you see it?" "Gertrude if you don't shut up, I...here it is. I found it."

Shirley made her way back into the room,

"I'm sure there's nothing to worry about, but just to be on the safe side, we'll make an appointment."

"Shirley..."

"I know you're scared Sissy. I'm here."

"Thanks Sissy."

As Shirley dialed the number, my heart raced...as did my thoughts.

> *"646-1591...Gertrude, everything will be...yes......*
> *Yes...Dr. Cruz? This is Shirley, Helen Smith's*
> *daughter...I'm fine thank you. Listen, I'm calling*
> *about my sister. I need to make an appointment for*
> *her to come in and see you. Yes, Gertrude...well,*
> *she fell today on her way home from work and has*
> *discovered a lump...knot of some sort on her breast.*
> *O.K....fine...that will be perfect. This evening at*
> *7:30pm...yes...thank you Dr. Cruz. We will be there...*

the family? Oh they're all doing just fine, thank you.
Yes we're all doing the best that we can. Yes, it's hard,
but we have each other. Thank You. We will... good-
bye."

"What did he say?"

"He'll see us tonight at 7:30pm."

"Tonight! You see, I told you it must be serious."

"Gertrude-"

"No Shirley. Why else would he need to see me so soon?"

"Stop it. Just *please* stop it. You...you just don't want to put these things off, that's all. It doesn't mean anything honey."

"I don't know what I'm going to do. I just don't want to-"

"Gert, I'm here. Whatever you have to do, I will be there right beside you. I know it's no use in telling you not to worry."

"Yeah, it's too late for that."

"Well, try not to worry too much then. Now listen...I have to run home, but I'll be back around 7:00 pm and Gert-"

"I know Shirley, I'll be ready."

Before Shirley left, she gave me one last look. It was her way of comforting me. "Gert...we will be just fine. Do you hear me?" All I could do was *force* a smile on my face and nod. The strength I found in Shirley's eyes helped to ease my nerves somewhat. I love my sister dearly. There's nothing in the world I wouldn't do for her and she me. As Shirley walked out the front door, I followed her down the walkway and into her car.

This was the last good memory I would have before my life changed. I would never be the same after my visit with Dr. Cruz.

CHAPTER FOUR

A Visit to the Doctor's

D amn it! Shirley told me to be ready and look at me...I'm still in my work clothes."

As Shirley pulled into the driveway next door to turn around, I began running frantically 'round the house trying to find my keys, my bag, and my comb. No matter how I felt, I had to make sure that my hair was looking good. There are many things that people can say about me, some good and some not so good, but the one thing they can say without a shadow of a doubt is that "Gert's hair was always together!" My hair was my pride and joy. I may not have a lot of money, but I was always taught that looking like a million dollars is free.

"Gertrude!" Shirley shouted from the car, "I told you to be ready. If you don't bring your-"

"I'm coming, Shirley. Hold your damn horses."

"You see, this is exactly what I'm talking about. I hate taking you anywhere. If I tell you to be ready-" I knew Shirley was hot with me. She hated waiting more than anything. "I said I'm coming!" I screamed out the front door. "I'm just looking for my bag."

"Your bag? What the hell do you need your bag for? Just grab your keys and come the hell on." Shirley was sure 'nough getting on my nerves. The last thing that I wanted to hear from her today was her mouth complaining about me not being ready.

"Look Shirley, if you can't wait, then go the hell on. I'm tired and in no mood for your *bossiness*."

"Gert, shut up and bring your tail on. It's hot as hell out here and you have me sitting in this car waiting on you. If I didn't want to take you, I wouldn't. Now come on."

"I'm just saying..." I said loud enough for Shirley to hear as I locked the front door. "I've got enough on my mind without you telling me what to do and how fast to do it."

As I got into the car, I was so angry that I couldn't even look at Shirley. She knew that the one thing I hated the most was being talked to like a child.

"What the hell were you doing in there anyway?" Shirley asked, as we drove off.

I said, "I couldn't find my bag. Damn..."

"Now you know as good as I, that you were combing that head in the mirror."

"I was not." I hated that Shirley knew me so well. I tried my damndest to keep a straight face, but soon broke out in hysterical laughter. "Girl, you know me like that back of your black hand."

"Honey, you and that head of yours. You're gonna be late for your own funeral." Both Shirley and I laughed so hard that we couldn't speak. "You ain't said nothing but the truth there Sissy. Besides, I told you that I want that Cookie girl to do my hair when I-"

I caught myself in mid-sentence. Although we were just joking around, it hit me like a ton of bricks. I was on my way to the doctor's to talk about the knot on my chest. This was serious and here we were joking around talking about my hair. I just didn't feel like laughing anymore. I focused on looking out the window, watching the cars go by.

"Gert...Gertrude don't you hear me calling you?"

"Sorry, Shirley, I guess my mind wandered off."

Shirley reached over and placed her hand on top of mine.

"Sissy, remember what I told you. I'm here for you no matter what."

"I know, Shirley. I know that you are and that I'm gonna be just fine."

"You don't sound too sure of that."

I moved my hand out from under Shirley's and placed it on my chest. "No, I'm not. The truth be told, Shirley, you're not even sure yourself. I don't think I can do this Sissy."

"You can and you will. I'm not gonna sit up here and let you bury yourself six feet under when you don't even know what's going on."

"Shirley, I know what I feel and-"

"That means nothing to me. We are not going on your damn feelings. We are going on facts and right now, we don't have them. "

As Shirley drove up to the front of Dr. Cruz's office, she was happy to see a parking space right up close. "Thank you, Jesus. Now I don't have to walk a long ways on these bad legs of mine."

"You talk about me? When are you going to see about those legs of yours?"

"I told you what the doctor said the last time I went. He told me that it's poor circulation. It's from standing on my feet all day teaching. Those floors are hard as hell." As we got out the car, we both had to laugh at ourselves. Both Shirley and I had to nudge our way to the edge of the car seat, rock back and forth until we got good momentum going, then slowly push off the car door to get to our feet. From there, we had to stand for a couple of seconds to let our legs adjust and then shuffle our feet slowly until we moved into a full stride. We had it down to a science. We couldn't move any faster than our bodies would allow us. I laughed to myself as I looked at Shirley cussing under her breath.

"I see you over there trying to act like nothing's wrong. Honey face it, you're old. You just can't do what you used to do and sure as hell how you used to do it."

"Oh shut up, Gertrude," Shirley laughed as she placed one hand on the car to rest.

"Sissy, you're just as bad as me. We both are old. Besides, if you don't look like Momma over there a huffin and puffin. You know you need your asthma kit. So why don't you just use it?"

"Oh hell. You think you're so smart. I was just reaching in my bag to find it."

I always struggled with Asthma. I took right after Momma. Sarah had a touch of it herself and Shirley, well as far as I could remember, she didn't have it. Once we got to the steps leading to Dr. Cruz's front door, we had to pause to catch our breath again.

"Damn it!" Shirley shouted.

"Shirley, there's no use in complaining. It sure won't make anything better.

"I know what you're thinking, Gert."

"You should. You were right there beside me." The last time that Shirley and I stepped foot in this office was when we brought Momma to see Dr. Cruz. She had grown tired and was feeble. The cancer had taken its toll on her and there was nothing else that Dr. Cruz could do but make her last days as comfortable as possible.

"Funny, you wake up each morning thinking that your day is going to be the same old uneventful day."

"I know, Sissy. I know."

"You never think that on this particular day, your entire life will be turned upside down."

"Gert, don't do that to yourself."

"If I had only been paying attention. If I had only just watched where I was walking, none of this would have happened."

"Gertrude, you can't blame yourself. What is meant to be is meant to be."

"So, it was meant for me to have cancer?"

"Now, Sissy, I didn't say that."

"Then what are you saying?"

"I don't know, sweetheart. I don't know why God does what He does. Besides, you don't know that you have cancer."

As Shirley stood beside me trying her best to be positive and supportive, I took one step forward and placed my hand on the door knob. I took in one deep breath and opened the door.

"We will see. We will see Shirley."

Once inside Shirley and I heard the familiar voice of Dr. Cruz coming from his office. He sounded like he was on the phone as usual, talking to a patient. Dr. Cruz was the family doctor. He had birthed many of the children running around Penllyn and cared for many of the sick. He was that doctor that you could call in the middle of the night and he would come running. We loved him for that. He cared about his patients and considered each his family.

Dr. Cruz must have heard us come in because as soon as we sat down, he opened up his office door and stuck his head out. "Uh huh...yes...okay. Well, tell your husband it is extremely important for him to continue his medication and if he does not get better in say about two to three days, he can make another appointment to see me. Gert, Shirley come on in. I'll be with you in one moment."

"That's fine, Dr. Cruz. We'll just sit here."

"No, no, please come on in and have a seat in my office. I won't be long. Besides, it's just Mrs. Johnson calling about her husband again."

"Dr. Cruz we'll just-"

"Now where was I? Oh yes. Mrs. Johnson, now we've been through this before...yes, I know Mrs. Johnson...yes, your husband is hard headed and stubborn...yes, I know he won't listen to a damn thing you say. Uh huh, listen Mrs. Johnson, I have other people here in the office that I must tend to. Mrs. Johnson, yes, no...Mrs. Johnson just have your husband call me if he needs to. Good-bye now."

I had to laugh to myself. Our community is so small that I knew exactly who Dr. Cruz was talking to. Mrs. Johnson is right. Her husband is stubborn and hates taking his medication. Not only did he hate taking his medication, he was just old and mean. I don't see how she stays with him. Well, I guess people said the same thing about me and my Fred...God rest his soul. He got on my damn nerves, but I miss him so.

"Shirley, Gertrude, I tell you, if people would just listen to their doctors and stop telling them how to treat what they think they have, my life would be so much easier. I spend the majority of my day listening to patients complain about being sick, not feeling good, not getting any better all because they refuse to follow my directions. How do you think you're going to get better without taking your medication? I'm the doctor." Dr. Cruz went on and on about his patients not listening to him.

I didn't come to the doctors to hear about other people's problems. I needed help myself. Shirley sensed that I was about to go off and knew that if she didn't do something quickly, Dr. Cruz was going to experience *the wrath of Gertrude Mildred Candie Cox Smith*. I didn't care if he was our family doctor. People are people and if you give them the chance to run all over you, they will. I just don't give them the chance.

"Dr. Cruz...Gertrude," Shirley interrupted as she placed her hand on my lap. I guess she thought that was going to calm me down. If anything, it just irritated me more.

"Oh...oh, I'm so sorry. Where are my manners? Please accept my condolences on the passing of your mother. She was a God-sent and will surely be missed. I tell you, the funeral was beautiful. Your mother would sure be-"

I just couldn't take it anymore. I didn't want to hear about Momma's funeral or his patients that didn't want to take their medication. Hell, I didn't even want to be at the doctors in the first place. I knew what was wrong with me and didn't need no doctor telling me something else.

"Dr. Cruz!" I screamed.

"Gertrude don't."

"Shirley...*you know me*. I can't take much more of this."

"Dr. Cruz, Gertrude needs to talk with you. We appreciate you seeing us at the last minute."

"I'm so sorry Gertrude. Let's see...oh yes, Shirley told me that you fell on the way home and found a-"

"A knot! I found a knot on my breast."

"O.k. Gert just slow down and tell me what happened."

"Dr. Cuz, I was on my way home from work and I didn't see the pothole in the road. I was thinking about Momma and before I knew it, I went right down. I fell on my chest and hands. After getting myself together, I made it home and noticed that my chest was hurting. The pain was unbearable, so I tried to lay down, but couldn't. I realized that the pain was coming from the left side of my chest, right above my breast. When I placed my hand on the area, I felt a knot. We just lost Momma to cancer and I don't want-"

"O.k. I understand. Well, let's take a look at it. Come on over to the light so I can see." I couldn't move. No matter how hard I tried, I couldn't get up from the chair. Shirley was on it. She knew me well.

"Sissy, I'm here. We will get through this together."

Shirley placed her hand on my elbow and stood with me. "One step at a time Sissy. Just take one step at a time."

"O.k. now let me have a look. Just relax as much as you can and stand up straight." I tried reading Dr. Cruz's reaction, but his expression was flat. There was no emotion...no reaction... nothing. How come I was the only one worried? I knew...I knew what was going on and didn't need Dr. Cruz to confirm anything. He maybe the doctor, but I know my body. Something wasn't right and he wasn't going to tell me otherwise.

"Now Gertrude, I'm going to pull your blouse back gently to have a look at your chest. All I want you to do is breathe for me. Can you do that?"

I could have busted him right in his mouth for saying some dumb shit like that.

"Breathe? Breathe? What the hell do you think I'm doing now?"

"Gertrude! Now, Dr. Cruz was kind enough to see you at the last minute and this is how you're going to thank him. Get yourself together!"

"Dr. Cruz, I'm-"

"Gertrude, I know you're scared. Please...it's o.k. All I want you to do is trust me. Now, let's have a look shall we?"

Once again, Dr. Cruz slowly unbuttoned my blouse and gently pulled it apart.

"Do you see? Do you see Dr. Cruz?"

Dr. Cruz didn't say anything. He rubbed his hands together and blew on them to warm them up I guess.

"O.k. Gert, now I'm going to press on your chest. Just tell me if this hurts in anyway." Shirley stood closer to me and held me around my waist. "Breathe, Gertrude, breathe."

"Oh!"

"You're doing just fine. You are almost finished."

As Dr. Cruz removed his hands, I fell back into Shirley's

arms.

"You did fine Gertrude. We're all done."

Shirley returned me to my seat and helped me button up my blouse.

"*Well???*"

I couldn't stand the silence. Someone needed to say something to me and in a hurry. Dr. Cruz just stared at me. He didn't say anything. He just looked at me.

"How is she Dr. Cruz?"

Just as Shirley asked, Dr. Cruz rose from his chair and walked gingerly to his desk. He reached behind and pulled open a drawer. As he turned to face me, I notice that he was writing something on a small card. My mind just raced with thoughts. No one was saying anything to me. I couldn't take it anymore.

"What are you writing on that card?"

"Gertrude, what I think we ought to do immediately-"

"Immediately!"

Dr. Cruz walked slowly towards me and with that same damn blank look on his face I said, "Tell me *something* Dr. Cruz. Don't just sit there writing on the *damn* card and not say one word to me."

"Gertrude, as I was saying before, what I think we ought to do is make an appointment to have some tests run to see what we're dealing with."

"No, you said immediately. Why immediately? Why?" Shirley walked to my side catching my attention. "Shirley..."

Without saying a word, she stood in front of me blocking my view of Dr. Cruz and that damn card and simply said, "I'm here Gertrude." I wanted to collapse. I wanted to fall right in Shirley's arms to be reassured that everything was going to be alright. I couldn't breathe. My chest was tight.

"Gertrude...you're getting yourself all worked up over

nothing. He just said that he wanted you to have a few tests done. Yes, he said immediately because he knows you worry. Why would he have you wait for a month to find out what's going on, knowing that you would go crazy waiting?"

Behind Shirley I notice Dr. Cruz standing in the background smiling. I wanted to ask him what the hell he was smiling about, but as soon as I went to open my mouth, he interrupted me by laughing.

"Gertrude, you haven't changed one bit. That mouth of yours and those eyes could kill someone in one split second. I remember your mother, God rest her soul, telling me all about that mouth of yours. She knew that she didn't have to worry about you one bit. You, of all your siblings, would be able to take care of yourself."

"That's right and don't forget it either."

"Do you remember the time when you were sitting on your mother's porch watching Brad ride his bike up and down the sidewalk and that boy...what was his name?"

"Stevie"

"Yes, Stevie...he told Brad that he better get his butt back across to his side of the street?"

Shirley turned to face Dr. Cruz and smiled. "I sure as hell do remember. I thought I was going to have to call the police to get Gertrude off that boy."

"Well, he had no business telling my Bradie where he could and could not ride his bike. Made me mad that's all."

"Before we knew it, you had jumped off the porch and grabbed that boy by his collar and dared anyone to say anything to you."

The way Dr. Cruz imitated me just made me laugh at myself.

"I don't know who the hell you think you're talking to, but if you don't get your narrow, black ass back on your side of the street, you'll wish you were never

*born. And if you think telling your mother is gonna
stop me, you're sadly mistaken."*

Shirley fell back in the chair laughing.

"Yeah honey, you were never scared."

"That's right. I said what I had to say and that was it. Beside, Bradie never bothered anyone. He was and is a good boy."

By this time, Dr. Cruz was standing beside me with a warm, comforting expression on his face.

"Listen to me Gertrude, they are just tests...just a few tests to be on the safe side."

As he placed the card in my hand, I focused on its sharp edges. I couldn't look at Dr. Cruz, but I needed to know.

"Do you think it's-"

"I don't think anything yet. Have the tests done and we'll go from there."

I couldn't help myself. I just started crying. I was afraid. "One step at a time Gertrude. One step at a time."

Shirley took the card from my hand and placed it in her purse.

"Shirley, I'll meet you at the car."

"Gertrude, you will be...*you are fine*."

I started to walk away, flooded with so many thoughts that I could barely see straight. "Gertrude, I'll be right there." As I walked out of the office, I noticed that Shirley was being held back by Dr. Cruz. I don't think that he meant for me to hear what he said to her, but I did.

"Call quickly. Your Sister maybe in serious trouble."

I couldn't pretend that I didn't hear what was meant *only* for Shirley's ears. I was never any good at faking or acting like everything was all right when it wasn't. My eyes fixated on the office door awaiting Shirley to come through. I didn't know what I was going to say or even if I was going to say anything at all. That would be too obvious. Me...ME not say anything?!

As Shirley appeared in the office door, I could see her eyes affixed on me. For some reason, I felt the need to comfort her. I felt the need to protect her even though I was the one who needed the reassurance. I could see her fighting back *what appeared to be tears* in her eyes. My sister loves me. She loves me enough to pretend like everything is going to be alright, when in fact neither one of us knew if that was the case.

As we got into the car, there was this awkward *presence*. It was like cancer was looming over us like a dark, rain cloud again. I recognized it. I felt it. I was familiar with its ominous presence. The entire way home I tried to imagine why Dr. Cruz said what he said. Why did he say it to Shirley and not me? It was my life that we were talking about.

"Gertrude..."

"Not now Shirley. Not now."

The ride home was painfully long. Trewellyn Avenue couldn't come any faster. I welcomed the church on the corner. I welcomed the little, nappy-headed boys walking in the middle of the road showing no respect for the car behind them. I just wanted my old life back and to forget this ever happened. Soon we pulled up to the house and parked the car in Ida's driveway. I shook my head as I noticed Sarah's car parked out front.

"Jesus..."

"Listen Gertrude, you're not alone. There is nothing to worry about. We will-" I couldn't bear to hear one more positive, motivating, inspiring speech come out of Shirley's mouth. I quickly jerked the handle on the car door and flung it open.

"I'll be inside."

I didn't mean to slam the door, but I did.

"*Sorry*," I said without looking back at Shirley.

Sarah had no idea what was about to take place. She was sitting on the living room couch watching television. I took one deep breath and opened the door. I had no idea if Shirley was behind me or not so I left the front door wide open. That should have been the first clue to Sarah that something was wrong. I never left the door open. I was constantly on the children for letting in flies and letting out all the cool air in the house. I probably yelled for them to shut the door and told them if they continued to do as such, the door would be locked and they would have to stay outside all day drinking water from the water hose.

"Hey there Sissy. Where's Shirley?" Sarah asked.

"Behind me."

By this time, Shirley had made her way up the walkway and into the house. I found myself resting at the staircase right at the front door.

"Lord, I tell you it's still hot out there."

"Honey who you tellin? I spent most of the evening chasing after that dawg on Pookie."

"She was here?" Shirley asked, as she made her way to the Daddy's favorite reclining chair.

"Yes indeed. She just left. I'm surprised you didn't pass Tee-Dee on the way out."

"Child, I could have, but...well...it was dark and you know me and driving at night."

"I tell you that Pookie is a handful. She runs up the stairs, knowing dawg-on-well that I can't climb those stairs like she can. By the time I get up there, she *done* pulled out all the toys waiting on me to clean them up."

Shirley and Sarah laughed to themselves. Sarah was right. Pookie is more than a handful and we *were* too old to run after a child. Most of the time one of us stayed upstairs while the other remained downstairs. Hell, I couldn't even begin to climb those stairs like Sarah does. I sat at the bottom of the stairs yelling up to Shirley, who most likely was upstairs, "Shirley here come Poo." Shirley was ready for her.

I could hear her telling Pookie,

"Poo, now you either stay upstairs or downstairs.
You gonna play around one day and fall right down
those stairs as fast as you're running."

Even though I was not in the best of spirits, I sat on the bottom stair listening to Shirley and Sarah.

"Girl, what you sitting so far away for?"

"She's just old and tired. You know we ain't as young as we use to be."

"Sissy, who you tellin?" Sarah said as she began rubbing her knees laughing to herself.

"Honey, I remember a time when we used to dance the night away."

"That was you and Gertrude. I wasn't much for dancing," Sarah said.

"That music would come on and we'd be off to the races."

"Yes indeed, you two could dance like no other."

"You two? Well if my memory serves me correctly...and I'm not so old that I can't remember anymore...you were out there with us. The Smith girls could dance them under the table."

"We sure could honey. That Century House would be jumping. We weren't even supposed to be down there. If Momma and Daddy-"

"What did he say to you?"

I could no longer pretend like everything was fine and that I didn't see anything. I was tired and needed straight-forward answers.

"Gertrude, please not now." Shirley knew that this conversation was inevitable. There was no sense in putting off what was bound to be a heated exchange. I wanted answers. I wanted straight forward answers.

"What did he say to you Shirley?"

"What are you talking about?"

"Shirley stop it! I'm no fool."

"No one is calling you a fool. We just don't need to have this conversation right now."

"It is not up to you to tell me when I'm gonna have a conversation. This is my life that we are talking about. So I'm gonna ask you one more time and I would like a straightforward answer. What did Dr. Cruz say to you?"

Sarah couldn't help but be confused. She had no idea what we were talking about.

"What are you talking about Gert? What doctor?"

"Listen Sarah, there's something that I want to talk to you about."

"Stop it Gertrude. Why get everyone all upset when you have no idea what you're talking about."

"The hell I do. *I found it. I have it*."

By this time, Shirley had stood up and made her way to the dining room to light a cigarette.

"*You found it? You have it?* What in God's name are you talking about Gertrude?"

I couldn't even look at Sarah. I was fixated on Shirley. Sarah stood to her feet and walked closer to me.

"I asked you a question Gertrude. You have what?"

"Listen Sarah, today, on the way home from work, I-"

"Would you just shut up Gertrude? I'm tired of your overreacting."

Without realizing it, I had pushed passed Sarah and made my way to the dining room.

"I'm not overreacting Shirley. I saw Dr. Cruz pull you back and whisper something to you. You have no right to hold anything back from me. You're not Momma."

"Don't you think I know I'm not Momma? There is nothing to worry about."

"Nothing to worry about? I found a knot Shirley and there's nothing to worry about?"

"*A knot*? Would someone please tell me what the hell is going on?" Sarah was upset. As she made her way to the dining room, Shirley took one last drag from her cigarette and put it out in the ashtray.

"There is nothing to worry about Gertrude!"

"Gertrude, look at me," Sarah shouted. "Tell me what the hell is-"

"Gertrude found a lump on her breast Sarah! There...are you happy?"

"Gertrude..."

"I found a lump Sarah. I found a lump on my breast." Saying it knocked the wind right out of me. All I could do was collapse and lean against the chair beside me.

"Gertrude...are you all right?"

"Of course she is. On the way home from work, Gertrude fell and when she got home, she discovered a knot."

"Oh no."

"Sarah, Gertrude is just fine."

"Stop saying I'm fine Shirley! You don't know that. You have no idea what the hell is going on with me."

"All Dr. Cruz wants is to have Gert complete a few tests. That's all. From there and only then will we know what is going on."

"I don't need any tests to tell me what is going on. I have-"

"I said stop it! Don't you say another word. WE WILL BE FINE!"

"Stop it!" Sarah shouted. "*Just stop it!*"

Before Shirley and I could say anything, Sarah grabbed her keys and ran out the front door. "Sarah, wait!"

"You see? This is the exact reason why I didn't want you to say anything."

"I know Shirley. I know. I'm just scared."

"Gertrude...Sissy, we will take it one day at a time and turn everything over to the Lord."

"Shirley, I don't want to die."

"That's good because you're not going to."

"Listen, I need some time to-"

"Gert, it's o.k. You need some time to get your thoughts together. I'm gonna head on home. I'll check back in with you a little later."

"Don't worry about me. I'll call you if I need you. I love you Sissy."

"Well, you may get the hell on my last nerve, but I love you too."

Shirley quietly gathered her belongings and walked to her car. As she drove off, I slowly closed the living room door and sat in Daddy's reclining chair.

"Lord...I know I don't call on you as often as I should...people think that I am tough and can handle anything. Well, the truth is...I need you. I'm scared Lord. I don't want to die. I know I have to be strong for my children, but Lord...how can I be strong for them when I can't even be strong for myself? I'm pretending Lord. I'm good at screaming and yelling... cursing and being angry, but I don't know how to...to be afraid. I'm not good at it so I just play it off like nothing bothers me, but it does. If only they knew what it was like to be me and have to hide. I just don't want to die Lord. I'm not ready. Will anyone be there for me like I was for them? Will they care enough about me to tell me, "It's gonna be alright Gert. Just you wait and see"? I'm losing control over everything and it scares me, I'm not sure if I can hold

it together much longer. Please send me a sign that
everything will be fine. I just want to hear from you
Lord. Please just let me hear from you."

I really needed to hear from God. I was desperate. As I glanced down at the coffee table, I noticed the card. It was the business card Dr. Cruz gave Shirley. When I reached to pick it up, my hands trembled.

"Get yourself together Gert. Get yourself together." As I look at the card, a sense of peace came over me. I can't describe what it was, but I felt *comforted*. I didn't need Shirley or anyone to call for me. Before I knew it, I started dialing the number on the card. "Hello...yes my name is Gertrude...Gertrude Cox and I was referred to you by Dr. Cruz...yes, well the reason I'm calling is ...well, I found a...I guess it doesn't matter why I'm calling, but...well, I have to make an appointment to come in and be seen by the doctor. Yes that's right. He recommended Dr. Young...Dr. Su Young. I need to see her as soon as possible. *It's an emergency*. Cancer...yes...I...did find a lump on my breast. What time can I come in? 11:00? No that's fine for me. 11:00am this Saturday. Thank you very much...you too...have a nice day. *Good-bye*."

CHAPTER FIVE

Good Morning God

Although I tried to get a good night's sleep, I just couldn't. I tossed and turned all night long, thinking about how my life was just turned upside down. I couldn't help but think about my family...my boys. I wasn't ready to die. Who would take care of my boys? Who was going to make sure that they would be alright? They needed their mother and I sure as hell needed them. Lord, I can hear Shirley already blaring in my ear,

> *"Gertrude, I wish you shut up with all that negative thinking. You're gonna talk yourself into an early grave. You just worry and worry and worry."*

She was right to some degree. I spent the majority of my life, if not all of my life, worrying about things that I just didn't have control over. That was just me, but sometimes people just walk around as if they have on blinders. They don't see all that is going on around them. I see it. I see it all and if they only knew like I knew, then they would worry too. Granted, I may take my worrying too far sometimes, but I just can't help it. Lord knows, there must be some kind of *medicine* out there to help with this sort of thing. Hell, I worry so much that I probably *would* worry myself right out of taking it.

I had to laugh to myself. - *Maybe there's something to what Shirley's saying after all*. Here I am lying in bed worrying about death, not even realizing that I am still alive...that I woke up this morning...that God has blessed me with another day. I guess it could be worse than what it really is. As my pastor says every Sunday, "*It could have went the other way*."

I tickle my own damn self. Worrying has been a part of my life for so long that I don't even know how to live life without worrying. Worrying is normal for me. As I laughed to myself, I just laid there staring at the ceiling.

I can't remember the last time that I just laid in bed instead of jumping up...making sure Bradie was off to school or had a hot breakfast waiting for him *or* something. Usually, we were all rushing out the door. Fred and I had to drop Bradie off to Momma's and then head off to work ourselves.

Boy...things sure have changed. Fred's gone. Momma's gone and now I'm facing...my kids are my life. Skippy's on his own and Bradie is about to leave and head off to college. They don't need me anymore. What am I gonna do with my life. I'm not used to *living* life. My life has always centered around taking care of others. Now that there is no one to take care of, what am I gonna do? I'm not even sure if I know *how* to take care of me. Since the fall, I had to take time off from working.

I hated not being busy. Yes, staying busy is my way of not focusing on the problems in my life. Worrying gave me purpose. I am a caretaker. People depend on me. I have to be strong...healthy. There is no time for being sick. I had to work. I need to work. My children need me!

"*Stop Gertrude...just stop it. You're rambling*."

My mind was off to the races again. I usually rambled like this when there was something heavy on my mind. Hell, I knew what it was. I was afraid that I was going to die. In my mind, I was staring cancer right in the face and it was looking right back at me.

"Cancer...me?"

No matter how hard I tried to make myself stop thinking about the possibility of having cancer, I couldn't. This was a real possibility. The hell with what Shirley and Dr. Cruz say.

"Test...just a few tests and we'll wait and see?"

They're not the ones sitting here waiting on the damn test! They're not the ones who will have to deal with being told *you have cancer*. They just don't understand! I have watched how cancer destroys a person; how it can strip a person of their dignity, their independence, and their pride. I have seen the look on Momma's face when Bradie had to pick her up and carry her to the bathroom because she was so weak and couldn't walk.

I was the person on the other side of the closed door with Momma, who had to change her diapers and wash her up like she was a child. It killed her to be so dependent on me. She tried. She tried so hard to help herself, but she just couldn't. She had no dignity left. She would just look out the window. Stare off until I finished what I was doing. I would always say to her, "*Momma, I'm almost done.*"

I hated it when she would cry. I couldn't tell if she was crying because of the pain that she was in physically or if she was so embarrassed at the fact that someone was changing her. I didn't want to treat her like a child, but the truth be told, she *was* childlike.

I was the one who bathed her, dressed her, put her to bed and started the same damn things over each and every day. I was the one!

I lived with cancer every day of my life; from Mae Mae, to Aunt Mable, to Ida, Bernice, and on and on and on. Cancer kills! I don't want to die!

"Damn it!" I screamed. "Not me!"

All I could do was scream, but screaming didn't help. It didn't change anything. No one heard me. No one *ever* heard me. They just assumed that Gertrude would be fine. Hell, they wanted me to be fine. They needed me to be fine. If I wasn't, then someone else would have to do the dirty work. No one wanted to do what I did. I didn't even want to do it.

Yes, I was good at it. Yes, I enjoyed making the sick and dying feel comfortable. I was the one who held their hand every step of the way. I was the one who called for the family when they died.

"Not me, Lord! Not me!"

I didn't ask for this. I didn't ask for any of this.

"Shit!"

My mind just seemed to wander; spinning around and around in circles. I'm so tired of wondering about what is going to happen to me. *What will become of my life if I have cancer?* This was never supposed to happen to me. This was not how my life was supposed to turn out. I know I'm not supposed to get ahead of myself and think the worst, but I just have this feeling, this horrible feeling inside me telling me that I have-

"Stop! Just stop it!"

*   *   *   *

The house was quiet. Too quiet, even for me. As I looked around the room, I never felt more alone. Sometimes it doesn't pay to put-on this front that you are so strong and that nothing affects you. People always think that I am fine and can handle anything. Well, they do because that's all I let them see.

I need people. I need to be comforted and loved. I need people to check in on me. I need people to ask, "Gert, you alright?" I need to know that people care enough to check in on me.

Without warning, the phone rang. "Damn it!" The ringing of the phone scared the hell out of me. However, I was glad to hear the jarring sound. I needed to get out of my head. As I sat up and made my way to the edge of the bed, I picked up the receiver and cleared *the coal* from the corner of my eyes. "Hello?" I said, clearing my throat.

"Oh, Shirley, I thought it was you. I couldn't catch your voice. What am I doing? Sissy, you know me, just-"

Shirley was no fool. She knew that whatever was about to come out my mouth was going to be a big ol' lie.

"Just...yes, I was worrying. I know. I know you told me not. Shirley, listen to me...yes you're right. I know I have nothing to worry about. Yes Shirley, of course you're right. Yes, Shirley, I am laying in the bed. No, I haven't gotten up yet. Yes, I know I need to get up and do something. Yes, Shirley, I know it will help keep my mind busy." I had to keep reminding myself that she was only trying to help, but if she said one more word, I was gonna *cuss her the hell out*. "Shirley...Shirley stop! You're right and I am getting up out the bed now."

I knew that if I didn't get out the bed or sound like I was getting out the bed, Shirley was going to remain on the phone until I did or drive up here and pull me the hell out of the bed.

"I'm up! I'm up damn it. Yes, I'll get dressed and go downstairs. I'll get a cup of tea and watch t.v. or something. Yes, I'll call you when I get dressed. Yes, yes, yes Shirley."

I couldn't help but start laughing to myself. "What am I laughing at?"

Shirley could hear everything.

"Honey, I was laughing at you trying to take care of me. What? Oh Shirley...you know you're good at many things, but taking care of the sick is not your strong suit."

She knew I was right even if she was going to argue me

down.

"Sissy, now look, I know you have a heart of gold and would do anything for me, but can you imagine bathing me or, God forbid, changing my diapers like we had to...I had to do for Momma? I know, right."

As I made my way to the chair sitting alongside my bed, I remembered caring for Ida when she was dying from cancer.

"Lord Shirley, do you remember the night you called yourself helping me take care of Ida? Honey, I never laughed so hard in my life. What do you mean, you don't remember? Girl, don't make me pee on myself. You know, I haven't made it to the bathroom yet. Sissy, every time you thought I was gonna leave you in the room with Ida, you were on my heels tripping all over me trying to beat me out the room. You'd tell me, 'Oh, I'll be damned if you're gonna leave me in here by myself and have her die on me'."

Shirley's thing was cooking for the sick. She would cook anything for you and as often as you needed her to, but that was it. She'd even sit with the sick, well, it just depended on how sick; not dying sick, but regular sick. It had to be daylight outside. Clothes did not have to be changed and that there was no chance in hell that they were gonna kick the bucket while she was by herself.

"Listen, Shirley, I'm gonna head on downstairs and get something to eat. Call me later or come on up and sit on the porch with me for a little bit. Yes, girl I know you won't be up until your stories are over. Yes, I'll call ya if I need you."

As I hung up with Shirley, I heard a knock on the door.

Damn it! Who the hell could this be?

I tried looking out the bedroom window, but couldn't see anyone. It wasn't until I looked out on the street, that I recognized Sarah's car.

As I lifted up the window, I screamed out, "Sarah, I'll be

right down. The door should be open."

Well, I guess the door was open, because I had just close the window, and heard Sarah downstairs, "Gert, it's me. You dressed?"

"Yeah honey, just getting ready to come on downstairs."

"Ok, I'm gonna hang some clothes out on the back line. Come on down and help me fold some of these clothes."

"Be right down."

Lord knows I didn't feel like no company and I sure didn't feel like folding clothes. Daddy was probably rolling over in his grave watching Sarah hang clothes out on the back line on a Sunday. He was a hard worker, but when it came to Sunday, he rested and you rested. You were expected to attend church and the remainder of the day was for family and friends. You visited the sick and shut in, ate a home cooked meal with the family, and then rested. You didn't wash clothes, play cards, cut grass, and definitely no hanging clothes out on the back line.

My Sundays consist of fixing a cup of hot tea, two pieces of dry toast and sitting in the dining room looking out the window. It doesn't sound exciting, but it sure made me feel good. If it was warm outside, then I'd sit on the front porch talking with Dottie or Bon from across the street. That's all we did.

Every once in a while someone would drive by and stop in front of the house and carry-on a short conversation. Usually, it was Bumpsy or Mary from down the street, or even Shirley, but only after her stories went off. You might even have someone from the church stop by. If they didn't see you in church, they would stop by to check in on you.

Now, I believe in God and love the Lord, but I just don't go to church every Sunday. I never have and never will. It just gets to me sometimes how people, especially church folk, can sit right in your face smiling, then talk about you like a dog behind your back. I'm the wrong one. Whether in or out the church, I'll tell you just how I feel about ya and if you don't like it, then the hell with you.

"Gertrude? Gertrude?" Sarah hollered as she opened up the back door. "*Gertrude-*"

"Sarah, if you holler my name *one more time*, I don't know what I'm gonna do. I'm sitting right here in the living room."

Just as I heard the back door close, the phone rang.

"Hello?" I said as polite as I could. I wanted to tell whomever it was to not be calling me so early in the morning.

"Shirley? Lord, Sissy, I just hung up from you. What's wrong?"

As I continued to listen to Shirley talk on the other end, Sarah made her way into the dining room.

"Lord, it sure is hot. Oh Gert, I didn't see you on the phone."

"It's just Shirley. Be with you in just a minute...yes I'm here. No need in yelling at me. I heard you the first time. No Sissy, I don't need you to make a special trip up here. I went ahead and made the appointment myself. When? This coming Saturday at 11:00. Oh hell, I sure forgot you said that you'd have Pookie. No, no, I'll find someone to take me. No, Shirley! I said I'll be fine. Besides, it's just too much to get Pookie ready and dressed. Shirley, I know I should have waited for you, but... now listen here Shirley...all right. I didn't answer the phone to start arguing so just go on and watch your stories and call me later. What? Yeah, honey I saw her walking down the street this morning. Sissy, she sure as hell looks bad alright. It's a shame what them drugs did to her. No, no I didn't talk with her mother today. Really, I mean what the hell can she do with her anyway. Alright, alright. Well, you asked me. Girl go on and finish watching your stories. You called me remember? Bye."

"You said that was Shirley?"

"Yes, and you know how she is about disturbing her and her

stories. Like I told her, she called me. I didn't call her. Come yelling at me thinking I give a damn."

"Gertrude, you know Shirley and her stories."

"Yes I do and that's exactly why I didn't call her."

"I tell you one thing, it's too hot to be hanging out clothes."

"Sarah, now you ought to know better. If Daddy was alive-" Sarah stood up at the dining room table shaking out a long white sheet looking out the window.

"He'd be turning over in his grave. I know, I know. I never understood what the big deal was anyway. When you look at it, you're so busy throughout the week so your weekend is spent running errands and doing all the things you didn't have time to do during the week. Sunday is quiet and the laundromat ain't crowded."

"I hear ya, Sissy.Lord knows I agree with ya. That was just Daddy's thing."

"Did I hear you say that Shirley was watching Pookie this Saturday?"

"Yeah. Tee-Dee and Kelvin are going out; quality time. Now I have to find someone to take me to my appointment. Here I call myself taking charge of my life and not letting this thing get me down and having to get these tests done stop me from living. All I want to do is forget about it all. Every minute of every second of my life is filled with doubt and fear. I know, I'm not supposed to feel this way, but I do. I just want to-"

"What time is your appointment Gert?"

"I made it for 11:00am. I knew Saturday would be a good day since Shirley's stories aren't on and now look at the mess-"

"I'll take you."

Sarah offering to take me to the doctors caught me off guard. I know she loves me and would do anything for me, but for some reason, I never expected her to take me to get my tests done. I just remember how she ran out the house when I told her about the fall and me thinking that I had... funny, I can't even find the strength to say cancer. I know it's not for sure that I have cancer, but I know my body.

"Thanks, Sarah," I said as I moved from the living room to the dining room to help fold the clothes. "I doubt it will take no more than an hour or so." Sarah turned her back slightly away from me.

"No problem. Gert?"

"Yes?"

"Oh, nothing." Sarah seemed distant from me now. Something changed and I couldn't put my finger on it.

"Sarah, what is it? You look like you have something on your mind." I don't know if it was something I said, or what, but as soon as I asked her what was wrong, Sarah grabbed the laundry basket and ran outside.

"Sarah..." Before I could get out another word, Sarah was already outside pulling more clothes off the line. She stayed outside for a minute or so and then came back in. She didn't look at me or say anything to me.

"Sarah? Sissy what is it?"

"I said nothing!"

Sarah was so focused on folding or trying to fold another sheet that she wouldn't even look at me. Since she looked like she was struggling, I moved closer to her to help. As soon as I touched the sheet, Sarah snatched the sheet from me and moved back into the living room.

"Sarah, what the hell is going on?"

"How's Brad doing? It's about time for him to graduate isn't it?"

"Honey, he's so excited. I try not to let him see how much I *don't* want him to go all the way to Atlanta. I'm just gonna miss him that's all. Anyway, he's excited and nervous-"

Sarah attempted to run out the house again, but this time, I grabbed her by the arm and blocked her from leaving. "Sarah, look at me!"

Sarah snatched away from me and turned her back to me.

"It's just the heat. Honey, I'm wearing myself thin. Listen, I'll be back-"

"Enough is enough, Sarah. Now I want to know what is going on."

"How are you dealing with all this?"

"With all what?" I asked her as I placed my hand on her shoulder turning her to face me. "Sarah, I'm not following you."

"You're so calm and you found...well, you found a lump Gertrude."

For the first time in my life I didn't know what to say. I didn't know *how* I was dealing with finding this lump. All I could do was look my dear sister in her eyes and see the pain staring back at me. She looked worn in the face. She tried fighting back the tears, but was unsuccessful.

"Never mind," Sarah said as she sat down on the chair behind her.

"I look at it this way: I'm scared, and no matter what the test says, I have to live. I have to live for myself and for my children. I'll be damned if anything will interfere with that. I'm scared. I am scared as hell. Do you hear me Sarah? I don't know *what* to think sometimes. I haven't slept well for the last couple of days and I can't keep anything on my stomach, but I have to fight for my life if the doctor tells me it's-"

"Gertrude *stop*! *Please Just Stop!*"

Sarah quickly stood up and started gathering her belongings. It was too much for her. To be honest, it was too much for me. As Sarah reached for the door knob, she paused and without facing me said, "You can't leave me Gertrude. You just can't."

"I'm not, Sarah."

"Don't say that when that's not in your power. Gertrude, I have so much on me. I just feel so alone."

"Sarah...God-"

"*Don't!*" Sarah slammed the door and never looked back.

"Don't what?"

CHAPTER SIX

Confirmation

I wish I could say that today was going to be just like any other day, but that would be a lie. The truth is my entire life could change at the mere flip of a page.

I didn't sleep well last night. I just tossed and turned all night long. My mind raced with thoughts about my children and family, even more than usual. I couldn't help but think about who would take care of my children when I'm gone. I know that I am getting ahead of myself, but there is a possibility that Dr. Cruz could come back, with test results in hand, to tell me that I am going to die. I was afraid that he was going to tell me that he had done all that he could and only time would tell. Usually that means that God would have to work a miracle.

I believe in God, but I haven't been to church in a long time and I haven't prayed to Him in even longer. Funny, it's just like the good old Reverend would say Sunday after Sunday, "Don't just pray to God in times of need. Pray to Him through the good and the bad."

Boy, was he ever so right. Being sick, or the thought of being sick, puts things, life or whatever you want to call it, in proper perspective. You just really don't know how powerless you really are until your life and time left to spend with your family and loved ones is at risk of being taken away from you. You realize that no matter how rich, old, young, famous, or alone you are, death will come a knocking for us all.

I cried thinking about the possibility of having to miss the most important years of my children's lives. It's just not fair. My children need me and I need them. I've wasted so much time on simple, unimportant things. So what if I have a closet full of clothes or whatever? I can't take it with me. They'll be here long after I'm gone and will mean nothing to nobody. But, I sure as hell can say that despite the many mistakes I have made in raising my children, they know that I did the best I could and that I love them.

I just wish that Bradie and Skippy would get closer. They need to love each other. I need to know that they will look out for each other.

Shit!

There's so much that I have to and want to do with my life. I've wasted a lot of previous time on stupid shit and now find myself begging God to give me a clean bill of health and another chance.

"Oh Lord, Sarah will be here anytime now and I'm still in my nightgown."

I must have talked her up, because no sooner than I thought about Sarah, her car drove up. "Jesus, I told her I'd be ready."

When I saw Sarah get out her car, I raised the window and yelled out to her, "I'm almost ready, Sarah. I'll be down in a few."

I had to laugh to myself. Even Sarah knew I wasn't going to be ready. She knows I'm late for everything. Shirley jokes with me and tells me that I'm gonna be late for my own damn funeral. I used to laugh when she would say that to me, but it's no laughing matter now. I can't die. I can't go anyway yet. I need to be here for my children!

*Please, God...if you're listening... Please just make
everything the way it used to be. I promise I'll start
going to church more often. Please, God! Please
make me better.*

"Gertrude. Gertrude, come on. You're gonna be late!" Sarah shouted from the bottom of the stairs. I knew I was gonna be late and didn't care. I didn't want to go, but knew that I had to go. My life depended on it and so did the well being of my children.

"Damn it! Get yourself together, Gertrude."

Before I knew it, Sarah was standing in the doorway of my room. I didn't even hear her climb the steps. All I could do was look away from her. I didn't want her to see the tears streaming down my face and the bags under my eyes.

"Gertrude, didn't you hear me call you?" Sarah quietly asked, as she moved further into the room. I couldn't even face her. I am the strong sister. I am the one that everyone comes to in times of need. I am the one who takes care of the sick. I don't need anyone to take care of me.

"Gertrude...Sissy, what's wrong?" By this time, Sarah sat next to me on the side of the bed. I know she must have been taken aback when she saw the expression on my face. I didn't have to say anything. My silence spoke for me.

"I'm scared, Sarah. I'm so scared. What if-" Sarah placed her hand on the side of my face wiping away each tear as they ran down my cheeks.

"I'm here, Gert and you have *nothing* to worry about."

"Oh Sarah...I *do* have something to worry about. I have a lot to worry about. I'm gonna find out today that I have-"

"Don't, Gert. Don't do it to yourself."

"Don't do what, Sarah?" Sarah quietly stood and walked away from the bed. She brushed her hand along the curves of the rocking chair by the window.

"Momma sure loved to sit in this chair for hours and stare out the window. She never seemed more at home and at peace then when she was rocking and watching the children play outside. Do you think she knew she was going to die? I wonder what she was thinking about during her last days."

I didn't understand Sarah's train of thought. She seemed so distant at times. I just didn't understand how she went from telling me not to do this to myself , to now talking about Momma. "I don't know Sarah, but she sure *did* like sitting in that rocking chair."

"I miss her, Gert. I miss her *so* much."

"We all miss her, Sarah. I wish there was something that we could do to bring her back, but it would only be for selfish reasons. I wouldn't want Momma to suffer like she did."

"I know, but it would be so nice to have her back with us again."

"Yes it would, but I'm afraid that just isn't gonna happen. We just have to learn how to live without her."

"Gertrude...I can't make it without you."

"Oh, Sarah," I said, as I stood and walked over to her. "I'm scared...really scared to go and get my tests done today, but I'll be fine. I'll be *just fine*."

Sarah turned cautiously to face me, without looking me in the eyes and fell into my arms. "What am I gonna do if something happens to you, Gertrude? I am scared, Gertrude. I am *so* scared."

"Listen to me. You just listen to me and listen up good. I'm gonna make it. No matter what the tests say, I'm gonna make it. This ain't my first time dealing with something difficult. I'll deal with whatever Dr. Cruz tells me, but I'll be damned if some cancer or anything else is gonna take me out of here before my time."

I gently lifted up Sarah's face, wiped her eyes, and smiled.

"Don't you know who I am? I'm Gert; tough as nails and don't you forget it." Sarah laughed.

"Yes, yes you are."

"Now come on and let's get this over with." Sarah went back downstairs and waited for me to get myself together. As soon as I heard her reach the last step, I placed my hand on the rocking chair and closed my eyes.

"Momma, if you can hear me, I need you. I'm scared Momma. So scared."

*   *   *   *

As Sarah and I drove to Dr. Cruz's office, our conversation was strained. Funny, both of us couldn't stand the silence, but neither of us knew what to say. I laughed to myself, as this was a first for me. I never was short on words.

"Gert? You okay?"

I didn't know how to answer Sarah. Inside I was torn up. My stomach was upset and my head was killing me. I was a wreck, but I couldn't let Sarah know. "Girl you know me. I'm doing just fine."

"You *wouldn't* tell me if you weren't. I know you Gert. I know you just like you know me."

I laughed to myself. Sarah was right. She knew me, but I still couldn't let my guard down.

"Sarah, go ahead with that mess. I'm fine. Test or no test, I'm gonna be around for a long time. I'll be damned if cancer is gonna cut my life short."

As we pulled up to the hospital, my heart raced even faster. It felt like it was gonna explode right in my chest. Well, I guess if it did, I was at the right place. Hospitals weren't my thing. I guess a lot of people could say that.

As Sarah parked the car and turned off the radio, we sat in

silence for a minute or so. My mind was telling me to get out the car, but my body wouldn't move. "Sarah...I can't...I can't seem-"

"Gertrude, I'm here. You don't have to put on *a* front for me. I'm your sister and love you with all my heart. I will not let you go through this alone."

"I know, Sarah. It's just...well, I'm frightened."

"I know, Gertrude."

"I hurt Sarah, you know? I'm not as tough as I pretend. Things hurt me. You may not see me cry, but I do. You know?"

"I know, Gert. I know." I grabbed Sarah's hand and squeezed it as tightly as I could. As I was about to let go, one teardrop fell on the top of my hand. Sarah was crying. All I could do was look at her and find strength in her.

"Would you look at the two of us; two grown-ass women sitting in a car crying. Honey, we're a mess."

"Sissy, you ain't said nothing but the truth."

"Come on and let's get this shit over with."

As we exited the car and entered the hospital, we were met by Dr. Cruz. "Oh, I hope we didn't keep you long?"

Dr. Cruz smiled because he knew that I knew that we did keep him waiting. "Oh, Gertrude, I just walked up. Listen, let me show you where you'll be changing and then I'll show Sarah to the waiting area." Dr. Cruz walked me to a small room where I was greeted by a small framed, young, black woman.

"This is Jasmine. She'll take good care of you, Gertrude."

"Nice to meet you, Ms. Cox. If you'll follow me, I'll show you to your room." I didn't even look back at Sarah. I just followed Jasmine around the corner until we were out of Sarah's sight. "She'll be fine. Right Dr. Cruz?"

"Sarah, your sister is very sick. I wish I could tell you that we have nothing to worry about, but-"

"Where should I wait?"

"Follow me Sarah. It's just around the corner." Dr. Cruz led Sarah to the waiting area and soon returned to my side.

"So tell me, how are you doing?" Sometimes, Dr. Cruz just gets the hell on my nerves. He knows how I am. He knows that asking me a dumb ass question about how I am is only gonna make me go the hell off on him.

"How do you think I am?" I said as I looked him dead in his face.

"I'm sorry, Gertrude. I know this must be a difficult time for you-"

"No, you don't!" I knew I was wrong for snapping at Dr. Cruz that way. I felt bad, but I couldn't get mad at something that I wasn't able to see or touch. Dr. Cruz was there. I didn't mean to take it out on him and he knew that.

"I'm sorry, Dr. Cruz. It's just-" As Dr. Cruz pulled up a chair beside me, he looked me in the eyes and smiled. "I'm here, Gertrude. If you need to scream, yell, cry...whatever, I'm here and I'm not going anywhere."

"I don't cry!"

"Yes you do," Dr. Cruz said, as he laughed at my ridiculous statement. "You're human Gertrude. I know sometimes it may not feel that way or maybe you don't have the time to show that you're human, but at the end of the day, when you are all alone, you hurt, you feel, you cry."

"You think you know me don't you?" I couldn't help from laughing at myself. He was right. Throughout the majority of my life, I was the strong shoulder that everyone leaned on. I eased the pain of others. I never made time for me. If I felt the need to cry, I just brushed it off and kept it moving. Just as soon as I thought about how lonely I am sometimes, I started choking up. I didn't know what to say.

Dr. Cruz just smiled. "It's okay, Gert."

From that moment on I don't remember much. Things were

kind of in a haze. I just remember people in white robes calling out my name and telling me where to stand; how to stand, and some other things. It's funny how your mind knows what's best. I guess I went into shut down mode and just did what I had to do.

Before I knew it, Dr. Cruz was walking me out of the examining room and towards the room where Sarah was waiting. Sounds were muffled and things blurred as we walked down this long hallway. It's funny, as soon as the door opened to where Sarah was waiting, things became crystal clear.

"Alright Gertrude, you just go on home and as soon as I get the test results back, I will call you. I know it's worthless to say this to you, but please don't worry. Whatever the results say, you will be fine."

Me, not worry? Who the hell does he think he's talking to? That's all I do and I do it pretty damn good if I may say so myself. "Thank you, Dr. Cruz."

"You're welcome, Gert."

"No, really. Thank you."

As Dr. Cruz shut the door to the waiting room, I felt Sarah's hand grab mine. Without having to turn around, I could tell just by the way Sarah was holding my hand that she was worried about me. "I'm okay, Sarah."

"No, you're not."

"No...no I'm not. I pretend like I'm not worried, but I can't help but think about how my life will be if I find out that I have...we just buried Momma and...anyway..."

"Gertrude, I wish I could say that I would be as brave as you. I wish I could say that God will provide. I wish that I could say so many things, but know that I understand. I really understand. Know that I'm always here for you."

"I know. I know, and I love you for it. You just never know what you would do until you're in the situation; until it happens to you. I know that you're doing the best that you can to be supportive, but...well...it's my life. At the end of the day Sarah, it's my life.

I don't remember the ride home or the weeks that immediately followed. I went on with my life as best I could. Funny, there are so many things we don't know about that could be killing us right now, but because we don't know it, *we keep on living*. The very moment we find out that there is something wrong, we stop living. What the hell! You're gonna die from something anyway!

It must have been about two week later when I was sitting at home, settled in for the evening when the phone rang. I thought nothing of it. How many times a day does the phone ring and I just pick it up and start talking? This time was no different.

"Hello? Well hello, Dr. Cruz, how are you? What can I do for you?" I hadn't even thought about the test results. Funny, the last time that I even gave them the time of day, was when I was taking the damn test. Dr. Cruz said that he would call me when they came back and he sure enough did. "They did?"

It's just not fair. Just when you try to move on in life, something comes along and blows everything to hell. I tell you, it's just not fair!

"When can I come in? Well, Dr. Cruz I-"

I could tell in Dr. Cruz's tone that he was trying to tell me something without telling me. Maybe it was just my overreacting, as Shirley always says that I do. Or maybe he didn't want to tell me over the phone that I had it.

"Um...listen, Dr. Cruz-I see. Okay, Dr. Cruz, okay! I'll get someone to bring me in sometime. You need me to come in as soon as possible? Listen, Dr. Cruz, why don't you just come on out and tell me what the hell you are so desperately trying not to? Okay, okay...I'm sorry. I'll get Shirley or Sarah to bring me in. Fine! Dr. Cruz...don't let me die."

Gertrude just get yourself together. You don't know what Dr. Cruz has to tell you. Maybe he just wants to tell you in person the good news. Maybe he just wants to see the look of relief on your face when he says-

"God!" I got to call Shirley. I got to call Shirley! All I remember is picking up the phone and dialing so fast. I didn't even look at the number. "Come on...come on and pick up the damn phone. Pick it up! Damn it! Where the hell is she?"

Okay, just calm down and...call Sarah...that's what you can do. Just call Sarah. 643-25...25...25...oh what the hell!

What the hell is her number? I call her every day and now when I need to remember the damn number, I can't. 643...643... oh yeah...2514. Pick up the phone Sarah...pick it up.

"Sarah? Sarah, listen, please just listen to me. No, I'm not alright. Dr. Cruz just called me and well, he wants me to come in as soon as possible. Yes! The test! The damn tests are back. I'm trying to calm down, but I can't!"

Before I knew it, Sarah was walking through the front door breathing heavily. "Gertrude? Gertrude, where are you?"

"I'm here." I was sitting in the corner of the dining room staring out the window. Sarah just stared at me. She didn't know what to say and I didn't know what to do.

I guess I should be grateful that I don't remember much about the car ride to Dr. Cruz's. I don't think much was said. There was no radio playing, no talking, and no laughter. All I can remember is the sound of the wind being forced through a very small crack in the window. It was painful to hear. I don't remember parking or getting out the car or even waiting for Dr. Cruz in his office. All I remember is hearing, "It's cancer Gertrude. I'm sorry, it's cancer."

There's something about confirmation. I wondered how I was going to react to hearing that I have cancer. I thought I was going to scream and holler or even run out the room. I didn't do any of that. I just sat there looking at Dr. Cruz, shaking my head. "It's ok...it's ok...I'll be-"

"Gertrude, honey there's nothing to worry about. I think we caught it in time."

"God, what am I going to do? Who's going to look after my children? Who's going to make sure they're...I don't want to die!"

I didn't realize that Sarah had gotten up and walked over and sat in a chair in the corner of the room. I didn't think it strange or out of character for her to do so. She was always a private person and would always run out of a room or avoid having conversations letting us know how she was feeling. "No one said anything about dying. Now just stop it!"

"I don't want to die. I don't want to die. Please Dr. Cruz, please don't let me-"

"Stop it!" Sarah screamed from the corner. "Just stop talking about it!"

"Now everyone just calm down. No one's going to die and that's that. Gertrude look at me. Look at me!" I was so out of it. I couldn't think. Dr. Cruz placed his hand on my face and made me look at him. The tears just ran.

"Gertrude, we will get through this together. Now listen, I went ahead and made arrangements for you to be admitted to Montgomery Hospital immediately."

"Immediately? What? Why so soon?"

"Gertrude, it's serious, but we will do all we can to-"

"I'm gonna die!"

I could hear Sarah crying. I didn't have the strength to comfort her and think about me. I needed Shirley to be here. She would make everything alright. She *always* knew what to say. She always made everything better.

"Gertrude, honey, we need to operate."

"Operate!"

"Yes Gert, operate. Listen, I promised you that I would always be honest with you. I'm not going to tell you that the road ahead of you will be easy because it's not. Chemotherapy and radiation is hard on the body. Now we will treat this cancer aggressively."

"Oh Lord; chemo, radiation...why Lord? Why?"

"Gertrude, I will be there every step of the way. Do you hear me?"

"Yes, I know you will. Uh...listen, Dr. Cruz-um I have to go home and get some things together. Sarah, I'll meet you in the car."

Everything around me seemed to be moving in slow motion except my thoughts. My mind was racing. I even started thinking about my funeral and life after I was gone. *Who would attend my funeral and what would they say? Would my children be alright? Would they be there for each other?*

I know that Skippy and Bradie don't see eye to eye, but they are brothers. Hell, eye to eye is an understatement. You couldn't put those two in a room alone for more than a couple of seconds, before someone was screaming and cursing. Who was going to fix that? Someone needs to be there to remind them of the importance of family and that they only have each other. I wasn't going to be there. I wasn't going to be there.

I don't remember walking to the car or even noticing that Sarah wasn't right behind me, as she usually was. She hated doctors and hospitals. She hated them all. I didn't even have the strength to stop and turn around and look for her. If only I did, I would have seen Dr. Cruz pull her back and stop her from running after me. All I cared about was making it to the car and sitting with my intrusive thoughts.

"Sarah, your sister is going to have a long, rough road ahead of her and she will need all the support that you and the family can give."

"I know, Dr. Cruz. I know." If I had only stayed back, I would have seen Sarah's sense of urgency to not be alone with Dr. Cruz. I just didn't pay attention. "Dr. Cruz, I have to go. Gertrude needs me and...I just have to go."

"Sarah, how have you been? I haven't seen you since your last-"

"I'm fine Dr. Cruz. I'm fine. There's no need to keep asking me how I'm doing. I am..."

Sarah pulled away from Dr. Cruz and rushed out the office almost tripping over her own feet. What was her sense of urgency? "Sarah, please-" It was too late. Sarah had already made it to Dr. Cruz's front door and slammed it shut.

As Sarah and I pulled up to the house, Shirley was just shutting the front door. I barely let Sarah stop the car before I opened the car door trying to stop Shirley from leaving. "Gertrude, wait!" Sarah screamed as she slammed on the brakes.

"Shirley! Shirley!" I hollered from the end of the walkway.

"Where the hell have you two been? I called and called and no one answered. I thought something had happened."

"Oh Shirley...Shirley..." I rushed right past Shirley and into the house. I know she must have thought I was crazy or something. Here I am calling her name and running past her, almost knocking her over. I needed the comfort of my home. I needed to feel Momma's presence. I needed to shut the world out and just withdraw into my own private, secluded mind.

As Sarah parked the car, Shirley looked to Sarah for some clarity. Sarah just waved Shirley back in the direction of the house. Sarah could no more talk about what just happened than I could. When Shirley walked back in the house, she found me sitting in the den with all the lights out. No one ever sat in the den. There was no particular reason, but no one ever sat in the den.

"Sissy, what...what's the matter?"

In the den on the walls were pictures of all Momma's grandchildren and great grandchildren. I smiled as I looked at the pictures of Bradie and Skippy. "Do you remember this one?" I asked as I pointed to Skippy's graduation picture from Millersville University.

"We didn't know until the last minute whether or not he was going to graduate."

"Gert-"

"Oh, and this one of Bradie? He must have been in kindergarten. He looks so adorable in his yellow turtleneck and argyle vest. I'm so proud of the both of them." Shirley slowly sat down beside me and just listened.

"I know I made many mistakes with the both of them. I know that. I just hope they know that I did the best that I could. It's not easy raising children. There's no book to tell you what to do and not to do. You just do."

"Gert-"

"Oh Lord, would you look at this? I love this picture of Momma and all her sisters. They were all over Aunt Mabel and Uncle Willy's. I miss her."

"I miss her too Sissy." By this time, Sarah had walked into the house and found her way back to the den. Shirley glanced at Sarah and could tell that she had been crying.

"Would someone please tell me-"

"I have cancer." I didn't even look at Shirley. There was no screaming or shouting or falling out. I just said it. I just sat on the couch looking at the pictures.

"Cancer? What the hell is going on?" Shirley looked at Sarah for some sort of help. All Sarah could do was nod her head to confirm what she had heard.

"Shirley, I have cancer and they want to take my breast off. What am I going to do?" I slowly dropped my head and leaned back into the couch.

"Gert...Sarah...would someone please just tell me what the hell is going on? Cancer? You don't have cancer. I told you to stop all that overreacting. Just-" Sarah put her hand up and caught Shirley's attention. She just looked at Shirley.

"My tests came back and, well, Dr. Cruz sat me down and told me that I have breast cancer."

"Oh no...no Gertrude, there must be some mistake. We'll need to get a second opinion. There is some-"

"Stop!" I screamed. I wasn't screaming at Shirley, but I just needed her to stop. I appreciated her willingness to look on the brighter side of everything, but the fact is I have cancer. "I have cancer and no amount of screaming, yelling, and praying or anything is going to change the fact that Gertrude Cox has cancer."

Shirley covered her mouth and sobbed for just a moment. "Well, what did he say?"

I lifted my head and looked Shirley directly in the eyes. "I have to be admitted into the hospital immediately. He wants to take my breast off and give me chemo and radiation."

"Why so soon?"

Sarah leaned against the wall and said, "It's serious, Shirley."

I looked at Sarah and smiled. "Yeah...yeah, it's serious. I know. What am I going to do?"

Shirley exhaled and grabbed my hand. "We are going to be fine."

"I don't know, Shirley-"

"Stop. I said we are all going to be just fine. We have each other and will get through this together."

"Oh, Shirley," I sobbed uncontrollably. "what am I going to do? What am I going to do?"

Shirley pulled me into her arms and I just sobbed. "It's going to be okay, Gertrude. Just go ahead and let it out." Without warning, Sarah screamed so loudly that it startled Shirley and me.

"Stop it! Just stop it! I can't deal with this! With all this... God!" Sarah had run out of the house screaming and yelling at the top of her lungs. I know the neighbors heard her, but by the time Shirley and I made our way to the front door, Sarah was gone.

"Sarah..." I whispered.

"What was that all about?" Shirley asked.

"I don't know, Shirley. I don't know."

"Come here Gert." Shirley said as she sat me down on the couch. "Okay...so you have to be admitted tonight?"

"Well, Dr. Cruz said immediately. I assume that means tonight. Oh, I don't know Shirley."

"Fine, fine...there's no need to worry, I will call Dr. Cruz and get all the details. You'll be fine."

"Shirley?"

"Yes"

"What am I going to tell-"

"Brad will stay with Georgie and me for as long as needed."

"I don't want him to know that I have-"

"Gert, we'll tell him that you have some sort of...of female problem and that you have to go into the hospital for a while and that he will stay with me. Don't worry Gert, he'll be fine and so will you."

"I love you, Sissy."

"I love you, too."

CHAPTER SEVEN

There Is No God

A ny moment now, Bradie would be walking through the door smiling and asking me how my day went. How was I going to look at him and tell him that my day was just like any other day, when I knew damn well that it wasn't?

My job as a parent is to protect my children from any and all dangers. I didn't want my children to have to worry about anything other than making good grades and being the best that they could. Nothing was going to stand in the way of me giving my children the best life that I could and the best life that they deserved.

I don't care if I have to work three jobs. I don't care if I have to swallow my pride and wash the asses of all the white folk that call me "girl","hun", and even "nigger" to make the money that I needed to provide for my children. That's my job. The last thing that my children would have to do is worry about me.

It was killing me inside to know that I was going to lie to my child's face, but Bradie is not as tough as Skippy. He's kind hearted and would give you the shirt off his back. His eyes aren't open to the ways of the world as Skippy. Skippy is street smart and sure as hell can take care of himself. I don't have to worry about him. He will be more than fine, but Bradie? Bradie needs me to protect him. If he found out that I had cancer, I don't know what he would do. He would probably worry himself sick and I couldn't do that to him. After all, his life was just beginning. I know Bradie. If he found out that I was sick, he would sacrifice his dreams of going to Morehouse and stay here to take care of me.

The closer it got to the time when Bradie was supposed to get home, the more my heart raced. I pray that God just keeps me a little while longer to see Bradie get on his feet and to be able to take care of himself. After that, if He calls me on home, I'll gladly go.

I done told Shirley and my children over and over again that I don't want to be hooked up to no machine keeping me alive. Just let me go. I told them. I know that they are not gonna listen to me, but I just don't want to be no burden on anyone. Just let me go.

My thoughts were interrupted when I heard the front door open. "Bradie," I called out from the kitchen. "Is that you?"

"Naw Sissy, it's just me." Shirley had to run down to her place to check on the mail. She was expecting some money to come. She told me that she was gonna come right on back up and sit with me awhile.

I know she was only coming back up to check on me. Shirley didn't want me to be alone, especially knowing that I had to tell Bradie about going into the hospital this evening. She knew I was going to struggle with keeping my emotions under control and not to let on that Mommy is sick.

"Gertrude," Shirley hollered from the living room.

"Gertrude! Come on downstairs."

Shirley knows me well. Usually, I am upstairs sitting in the back room, just like Momma, looking out the window. The only other place I could be, if I wasn't there, was in the kitchen heating up some hot water for a cup of tea and waiting for two pieces of toast to pop up. "I'm in the kitchen. I'll be right out."

After turning off the whistling tea kettle and placing the two pieces of dry toast on a plate, I turned and met Shirley who was now sitting in the dining room smoking a cigarette. "How ya feeling?"

"Girl, my mind is all over the place. I'm just a mess."

"Gertrude, we just have to accept the fact that we are old and sooner or later, we are gonna get sick."

"Hell, Sissy, you don't have to tell me that I'm getting old. I know I'm old. Hell, I can *feel* it."

"Who you tellin? My knees ached so bad last night... all I could do was rub'um."

I laughed at the thought of Shirley and me getting old. We would be two old fuddy-duddies sitting together, keeping each other company. "Lord, won't that be a sight to see? You and me sitting together with our walkers."

"Now, I tell you one thing. I better hope that you don't get sick *before* me, 'cause if it was left up to Georgie, I'd be in a home."

"Shirley, don't say that."

"Honey, it ain't no secret. Georgie would spare no money in the matter. He'd put me up in a nice home and come to visit, but taking care of me...hell no."

I laughed to myself, listening to Shirley as she talked about being put into a home. Now don't get me wrong, Georgie loves his mother to death, but he'll tell you that taking care of the sick the way we do, is not his thing.

"Child, it ain't easy taking care of the sick. You have to be called to do it."

"You ain't said nothing but the truth Gert. I know he wouldn't do it, because I wouldn't do it. He's just like his mother. Now, I will cook all the meals, wash and dry all the clothes. However, changing diapers, giving them a bath, combing their hair, and changing their clothes is not for me. It's just not a strength of mine."

"I know, Shirley. It's hard on the body."

As Shirley and I continued talking, I heard laughter coming from outside. It was a good idea for Shirley to come back up, as she helped me pass the time away and not to get stuck in my thinking.

As soon as I heard the children walking down the street from the bus stop, I immediately fell back into my old ways of thinking. I knew that it would be only a matter of time before Bradie would burst through the door. I hadn't spent any time thinking about what I was going to tell him. I had to tell him something, but what was I going to say?

"Gert, take a deep breath. Everything will be just fine."

"I don't know Shirley. I mean, I *am* going to lie to my child. I mean, suppose he finds out the truth and never forgives me? How would I explain to him that I was only doing what I thought was best for him? I was only trying to protect him. What if-"

"Don't go there Sissy. We know our children. We know what they can and cannot handle. You know that Bradie would worry about you and he would give up all his dreams to stay here to be with you. You're doing the right thing."

The front door swung open and in walked Bradie. I was frozen. I know I had a look of utter fear on my face. No matter how hard I tried to think of something else, I just couldn't.

"Mom? Mom," Bradie called out from the living room. I looked over at Shirley and shook my head.

I couldn't say anything. I couldn't move. I just couldn't do anything.

"*Hey hunie*," Shirley called out from the dining room table. "We're in here."

"Oh, I didn't see you. How's everything?"

I took in a deep breath, but no sound came out. Shirley was so in tune with me. She knew that she only had a couple of seconds to say something before Bradie caught on that something was wrong. "All is fine Brad. Your mother and I were just sitting around shooting the breeze."

"Hey Mom, what's up?"

"Oh, I'm good. How was your day?" Brad dropped his book bag at the bottom of the stairs and came over and hugged Shirley, then me.

"Mom! I just can't believe it."

"You can't believe what?"

"I can't believe that twelve years went by *so fast*. It just seemed like I was in junior high school and now I'm about to graduate."

"Can you believe it? Honey, Mommy is so proud of you."

"I mean, I'm excited about going, but you'll be here by yourself. Who's gonna look after you when I'm gone? I mean, suppose you get sick and need to go to the doctors? Who's gonna be here for you?"

"Oh Bradie, sweetheart, don't you worry about me. I'll be just fine." Bradie walked over to me and just stared at me.

"Sweetheart, please don't worry about me. You know Mommy is tough and can look after herself."

"And you know Brad, I'm still here."

"I know Aunt Shirley, but I just worry. That's all."

"There's nothing to worry about, Brad. Mommy is fine."

"I know Mom. Just know that if you want me to stay here and-"

"Stop all that talkín crazy. I would never ask you to stay here for me. Of course, I'll miss you, but it's not like I won't see you ever again." I almost choked on the lump that formed in my throat. Just the thought of not being able to see my children again brought tears to my eyes.

"I love you, Mom."

"I love you, too." Bradie sat down at the dining room table and smiled. He almost seemed relieved that I didn't ask him to stay here in Pennsylvania. Although I did want him to stay; not because of me being sick, but because I was going to miss him.

"So, what did you guys do today?" I looked at Shirley.

"Well, honey, you know. Same old same."

"Yeah, I know. Not much changes around here. That's one of the main reasons why I want to move to Atlanta."

"Listen, Brad, there's something that I want to tell you, but first Mommy needs to let you know that she's fine." Although Bradie may be innocent and naïve, he's by no means dumb. He knew something was wrong.

"What do you mean everything is fine?"

Shirley cleared her throat to get my attention. She knew that I was beginning to panic. "Just that, honey. Everything is fine."

"Every time someone says that they are fine, they're not. So what's the matter?"

"Brad, your Mom has to go to the hospital this evening."

"This evening? What?"

My motherly protective instincts immediately kicked in. I wanted to make everything better. I wanted to protect my baby from being hurt.

"Bradie, Mommy is fine, now just let me explain." Bradie wasn't buying it or maybe I wasn't buying what I was about to tell him. I began to tear up, so I turned my head away from Bradie and looked out the window.

"What your mother is trying to tell you is that there is no need to worry. She just has to go to the hospital this evening to have a simple procedure done."

"Procedure? You mean surgery?"

"Yes, honey. It's nothing complicated or that serious, but it needs to be done."

"For what?"

Shirley got up and moved to sit beside Bradie. "Brad, your mother has to have a simple procedure done that many women her age have to have. You know, we're getting older and...well, honey it's just not that serious."

"Not that serious? Well, if it's not that serious, how come she has to be there tonight?"

"Because Dr. Cruz knows your mother and how she will procrastinate. He went ahead and made the appointment for your mother. Now, she will be in the hospital only for a couple of days-"

"A couple of days? What? Why so long?" Brad ran over to me and grabbed my hand.

"Mom, are you alright? I'm worried."

"Oh honey, don't you worry 'bout a thing. Aunt Shirley told you that there's nothing to be alarmed about. Mommy is getting older and many women my age have to have this surgery, but I tell you this, Mommy will be just fine."

"Stop saying that!"

"Stop saying what?" I asked.

"That you will be fine. I don't believe you."

Shirley moved over again, to be right beside Bradie. "Brad, honey, look at me. There is nothing to-"

"To worry about, I know, I know. Everyone keeps saying it over and over again, but I just don't buy it. I know you are always trying to protect me. You wouldn't lie to me, Mom, would you?" He knows there's something wrong.

I sure as hell hope that I am making the right decision to not tell Bradie. Suppose something happens during the surgery? How in the hell would someone be able to tell him that your Mommy died?

I placed my hand over Bradie's and forced a smile on my

face, "I will be here for a long, long time. Mommy's not going anywhere. Do you hear me?"

"*Yes*...it's just-"

"Bradie, don't worry. I told you that everything will be just-"

Brad kneeled down and placed his head on my lap and sighed, "*Fine*..."

"Now, tell me all about your day."

Shirley smiled and politely excused herself. "Listen, I'm gonna head on down to the house to finish up a few things. Call me when you're ready and I'll come on back up and take you to the hospital. Oh, by the way, you will stay with Georgie and me until your mother comes home. So, just get a few things ready."

"Yes," Bradie said quietly.

As Shirley was leaving, Bradie lifted his head and looked at me, "You wouldn't lie to me, Mom, would you?"

"Honey, don't worry. Why don't you just tell me all about your day?"

My mind continued to race as I tried to think about everything that had to be done around the house for Bradie. Although he was going to stay with Shirley and Georgie, I was worried. No one knows your child like you do. Sarah said that she would watch him until Shirley returned from the hospital. I didn't know what was awaiting me, so Shirley said that she would stay with me as long as I needed her or until the hospital kicked her out, whichever came first.

The house was quiet, too quiet for me. Bradie was in the front room watching t.v. and I just sat on the edge of the bed in the middle room drifting off into space. I wanted to call out to Bradie and ask him if he was alright, but I didn't want to worry him anymore than I already had. Really, I wanted him to call out to me. I wanted him to come into the room and throw his arms around me and hold me and tell me that everything is going to be alright. I hated lying to him. I prayed that it didn't come back and haunt me later, but I had to do what I thought was best for me and my child.

"Brad...," I softly called out.

From behind his shut bedroom door, I heard him faintly answer, "Yes?"

"You okay.?"

He didn't answer right away which frightened me for a brief moment, until he cracked the door open. "I guess so."

Bradie slowly shut the door and went back into his room. It took all my strength not to run to his side and stare him in the eyes to reassure him that Mommy's gonna be just fine. Hell, who was I kid'n? I didn't know if I was going to be fine. For all I know-

"Gert, stop it!" As I composed myself, I heard Bradie say, "Mom is everything..."

"Bradie, sweetheart, everything is just fine. I told you that I'm okay so please honey just try to rest. Aunt Sarah will be here in a few to look after you so just go ahead and watch t.v. Mommy will be home before you know it."

"Will I be able to come and visit you?"

"Honey, you don't want to be bothered with coming to see me. Mommy wants you to focus on finishing up school and making me proud."

"But I *want* to come see you."

"Fine...fine... I'll talk it over with Shirley and see what she says. Maybe she'll bring you over one night after school. How about that?"

"Please don't forget."

"I won't sweetheart. Listen, why don't you go see Georgie for a while. There's no sense in you just sitting around, waiting for me to leave. Go on and I'll tell Sarah that you'll be down there and I'll have her bring your stuff down later."

"But I want to stay here and be with you."

"I know honey, but... *please* just don't worry about me. Go on and have some fun down Georgie's and I'll tell Shirley to bring you over to see me later on this week. Matter a fact, as soon as I find out the number to the telephone in my room, I'll tell Shirley to give it to you and you can call me anytime you want. How's that sound?"

"Mom, if you-"

"Brad..."

"I'm sorry. I'm just worried about you. Call me as soon as you can, please."

"I will, honey. Now run along." I know he didn't want to leave my side, but I had to get him out the house for his sake and for mine. I could feel me tearing up on the inside and I didn't want to worry him any further.

Just as soon as Bradie headed out the back door, Shirley pulled up and Sarah walked in. "Gertrude, Shirley's here."

"Coming right down. Okay, girl. Pull yourself together and get this over with. You gotta get back here and take care of your children."

I didn't have much to gather. I didn't know what to take, merely because I didn't know how long I would be in the hospital. So, I just took a small overnight bag and a couple of magazines. "Gertrude, Shirley said come on before it gets too late."

"Tell her I said I'm coming so don't rush me." As I gathered up my small bag and shut the bedroom door, I took in a deep breath and headed on down the stairs. When I got to the bottom step, I looked around the living room and smiled.

"You never miss something until it's gone."

"Gertrude, stop all that. Ain't nothing gone and you're coming back home, so please...please just stop all that talkin."

Sarah sat across the room from me and avoided making eye

contact. She just looked off somewhere into the kitchen. "Love ya, girl."

"Love ya too," she said back.

"Bradie is down Shirley's. Please watch over him for me."

"I will Sissy. I will. Now, please go on before Shirley loses her mind out there waiting."

I laughed to myself because Sarah was right. "Sissy..."

"Gertrude, I know. All I want you to do is get better. Now go."

"Love you."

"I love you, too." Didn't know what was awaiting me, but it was now or never. *Bless me Lord*, I smiled at Sarah and then shut the door and never looked back.

"Get better, Gert. Please just get better."

As Sarah shut the door and had time to collect her thoughts, she realized that this wasn't some kind of nightmare that she was dreaming. No matter how much she tossed and turned, no matter how loudly she screamed, no one was going to shake her awake. This was real. This was not some kind of sick joke that someone was playing. *People are dying! My family is dying! I'm... Shut up Sarah...*, she thought to herself. *...before you say too much*.

Sarah was never the kind of person who told too much about herself. Hell, she didn't tell anything. She was private and liked it that way. She kept her thoughts to herself and that's just how it was.

Sarah just doesn't let anyone in; not even her own family. She was afraid to let them in. This world can be cold. Once people know anything about you, they can...will hurt you. Sarah heard what the family and others in the community said about her when they thought she wasn't listening, *"What's wrong with Sarah? Why is she the way she is? She seems so strange acting?"*

They just didn't understand. No one understands what it's

like *being Sarah*. Hell, I didn't know what it was like being Sarah and I was her own sister. I often thought Sarah felt like she just didn't belong. She was always *up under* Momma. It must be tough for her now that Momma's gone. Damn it, it is tough for all of us, but Sarah had a special relationship with Momma. One I just never understood and *to some degree*, was jealous of. Sarah needed Momma to protect her.

Hindsight, I just was so *caught up in my own shit*, that I didn't allow myself to see and hear the truth. My sister needed me. She needed her family and perhaps, we were not there for her.

Sarah told me later about what happened when I shut the door to go to the hospital. I had too much on me...I should have listened and saw the signs. I was too busy being a big sister and telling her what to think, how to feel, and what to do. *Sarah, I'm sorry*.

I can still hear Sarah's voice in my head as she sat in the house alone after Shirley and I left.

> *"Momma...Momma, I miss you. I hate this house.*
> *It's just not the same. I'm not the same. There are*
> *too many painful memories. Everywhere you look,*
> *there are pictures reminding me that you're gone. I*
> *hate what cancer has done to our family. The one*
> *person that I could count on to make it all better was*
> *torn away from me. It's just not fair. I'm so scared*
> *Momma. No one understands me like you. You...you*
> *were all that I had. The world's against me and...Oh*
> *God Momma...Momma, I miss you. Miss you so much.*
> *It's so hard being here without you. I can't do this*
> *alone anymore Momma. I need you. You promised me*
> *that you would always be here for me. You're gone.*

I can't reach out and hold you anymore. You're not here to tell me that it's gonna be alright baby. I'm afraid to close my eyes Momma. I'm afraid 'cause when I open them, I can't see you anymore. I can't hold you. You're gone...gone...and I am all alone. God...God please give her back to me. She was all that I had. I am nothing without her. How could you take her from me? I hate you! I hate you God! I'm hurting so much inside and you don't give a damn about me. I'm hurting so much. Make it stop. Please make it stop."

I should have been there for my sister. She didn't have to keep all of that to herself. I know she's private. I know she would have felt like I was prying. I know! I know!

I...my baby sister was alone and didn't have anyone to hold her.

As much as I try to block it out, I could never stop the sound of Sarah's voice screaming inside my head.

It's killing me God. I hate you for giving me...for allowing... cancer. Oh God, I have cancer and you don't care! You gave this to me. I hate you! Momma! I have cancer! I have cancer! Take it away. Please just take it away. Who's gonna make it better for me? Please take it away... please. I dare you God...I dare you to take it away right now!

I pray that God forgives me for not knowing that my sister had cancer and was suffering all alone. I guess it really didn't matter. Everyone has their own process and deals with situations differently. I just wish I had the opportunity to tell her earlier that it was all going to be alright or at least *I* hoped so.

CHAPTER EIGHT

They Took My Breast

I could faintly hear Shirley singing something in the background. I couldn't catch all the words, but it was familiar to me.

"Cause she's my sister,"

Shirley continued singing over and over. *"Cause she's my sister."* Honey, I wanted to laugh my ass off. I hadn't heard Shirley sing since the Sunbeam days. She was always so talented. She could play the piano, she sang in the choir, went to college and didn't need no help from nobody. *"Cause she's my sister,"*

I didn't quite understand why things seemed so much in a fog to me. I was aware of what was going on around me, but things were moving in slow motion and sounded so far off in the distance. The last thing that I remembered was leaving Sarah at the house and hearing her say, *"Just get better Gertrude... just get better."* The next thing I remember was driving away, with Shirley. From there, things just don't make sense to me.

"Cause she's my sister."

"Shirley...Shirley...please stop singing that damn song. I know I'm your sister...Lord."

"Sissy, the Lord sure broke the mold when he made you."

"Ah, go to hell," I said as I laughed to myself.

"Ain't that something," Shirley said. "Here I am sitting beside you in the hospital and you're telling me to *go to hell*. Why I have a right mind to-"

"Hospital!?" I screamed. At that very moment, every memory of the past couple of months, days, seconds flooded my mind all at once. I remembered every painful memory. Just for one split second, I thought that it was all a bad dream.

"*No, it's not a dream*," I said to myself, trying to hold back from crying. There was no awaking from this nightmare. It was not until I placed my hand on my breast and screamed did I realize that my nightmare was a reality.

"Shirley! Shirley! Shirley!"

"Gertrude, what is it? Do you want me to call the nurse?" By this time, Shirley was standing up over the bed trying to stop me from losing my mind.

"Oh God! Oh my dear sweet Savior!" Shirley tried her best to hold me down in the bed. "Gertrude, honey, you're gonna have to calm yourself before you pull all these tubes out of you." "Get off of me! Please just get off me!" I screamed begging Shirley to let me go.

As Shirley continued to pin me down, she accidentally placed her hand on my chest. "My God!" I yelled. "God, no... no...no!"

Finally, Shirley just let me go. I saw the pain in her face. There was nothing she could do to prevent me from having to go through what I was about to experience. All she could do was sit back and pray for me. "My breast...my breast," I screamed over and over again. "Oh God, no! Please God, please, please-"

"Gertrude, Sissy, you've got to calm yourself. Please just lay back and try to relax honey." Shirley did all she could to get me to calm down, but I wasn't having it. "No...no...no! You tell me what happened to my breast. Tell me!"

I can count the amount of times that I've seen my sister cry. Shirley was a rock and was always in control of everything. Even when Daddy and Momma died, she cried only just a little and went right back to being the pillar of strength for everyone. "Gertrude, sweetheart-"

"No, Shirley...no!"

"Gertrude, Sissy, they had to remove your breast because-"

"No, Shirley! No!"

"Honey, you have cancer and the doctors thought it best to remove your breast." Just hearing the word cancer took the very life out of me. I just laid back in the bed and turned my face away from Shirley. "Why Shirley? Why?"

"Gertrude, the doctors believe that they caught it in time and got all-" "I don't want to hear it! I don't want to hear anything about what they thought. Just give me my...my...just give it back."

"Oh honey I wish-"

"They took my breast!" I screamed over and over again. "They took my damn breast from me!"

Shirley pulled the chair closer to the bed and just held my hand.

"My breast! My breast! Shirley, what am I going to do?" Shirley was never at a loss for words, but there was nothing she could say to make sense of all of this madness. There was nothing that she could say to make any of this shit better.

Everything just seemed to happen so fast.

Just yesterday I had my breast and now I'm being told that I have cancer and that they thought it best to take my breast.

This was my body.

No one had the right to take something that belonged to me. Cancer didn't have the right! The doctors didn't have the right! God did have the right. No one had the right!

"Please tell me this is some kind of mistake. Please tell me Sissy." Shirley just quietly hung her head and rubbed my hand. "Sissy, I am afraid-"

I pulled away from Shirley and turned on my side, staring at the wall.

"Damn it!"

"I'm here honey."

"Please turn off the TV."

"Gertrude, you can't sit here in silence. It's not good for you."

"Turn off the television!" I shouted.

Shirley did as I asked, just as a familiar voice was heard in the hallway outside my door. It was Reverend Jones. He was always at the hospital visiting the sick and shut in. Funny, I never thought the day would come when I would be the one being visited.

"Gertrude, do you want me to call Reverend Jones to come pray for you?"

"I'm dying."

"The doctors said nothing about you drying. Now, you stop that crazy talk."

"What am I going to do Shirley?"

"We are going to fight this thing together. That's what we're going to do."

"I can't Shirley...I just can't. I'm tired."

In one swift movement, Shirley stood up from the chair, grabbed my face and forced me to look at her. "You are not dying! Do you hear me? Do you? You are going to live and that's all that's to it. Now, I am going to get Reverend Jones and he's going to come in here and pray the life back into you."

"Shirley-"

"No! No! You are going to fight for your life. Cancer or no cancer, you are going to get through this. We're going to get through this!"

"Shirley, I don't want to die."

"Shut up! Just please...please, just stop it Gertrude." Shirley's strength was going to be enough to get me through this. It was going to be difficult, but I had to fight for my life. Shirley left my bedside to step out into the hallway to call Reverend Jones over to my room. I wasn't use to being prayed for or at least that I knew of. I was the one who took care of the sick and helped them to feel better. You just never know when you're gonna need someone...need prayer.

"Excuse me Reverend Jones."

"Shirley, what a pleasant surprise seeing you. I didn't expect to find you here. Is everything alright?"

"Reverend, it's Gertrude. We were trying to keep this quiet, but she really needs to hear from you." "Gertrude...she's here... in the hospital?"

"Reverend, Gertrude has breast cancer."

"What?"

"Yes, cancer. One day, when she was walking home from work, she fell and found a knot on her chest and before you knew it, she's having surgery, chemo, and...Reverend, she needs you."

"But of course. What are the doctors saying?"

"Well, they're pleased with the surgery and feel like they caught it in time. It's just...well, they had to remove her left breast and...well-"

"Say no more. What would you like me to do?"

"At this point, she needs...we need you to pray for us."

"Take me to her." As Shirley and Reverend Jones entered the room, tears were streaming down my cheek. The sight of Reverend Jones made me weep even more. It was like seeing my Daddy all over again. When I looked in his eyes, it just felt like everything was going to be alright. My body felt warm, as if God had placed His hand on me reassuring me that He was near.

"Oh, Reverend Jones. Reverend-"

"Gertrude, everything is going to be just fine. We serve an awesome God that promised to never leave nor forsake us."

"Why me? Why me?"

"Gertrude, I wish I had the answer to that question, but only God knows why He allows certain things to happen to certain people. But you have to rest assured that in the end, everything will be just fine."

"I don't want to die, Reverend Jones."

"Well, that's a good thing because we're not going to let you die." In that split second, Shirley slumped over in the chair and broke down crying. Reverend placed his hand on Shirley's shoulder and comforted her.

"Oh Reverend...don't let God take my sister from me."

"Shirley, that's not up to me. All we can do is pray for God to have His way and wrap His ever loving arms around this family in their time of need."

"Please pray for me Reverend...*please*."

As Reverend Jones and Shirley circled the bed and held my hands, I have to be honest and say, at that point in time, I doubted if prayer was going to change anything. I feared that what *was done was done* and all that I cherished and treasured in my life was going to be taken away from me *in the blink of an eye*.

I even questioned whether or not God existed. When things were going well, I never questioned God. Why was I doing so now? Perhaps it was because the uncertainty of life and the possibility of death were at hand. This was no game. This was not a joking matter. This was my life and it was being determined by someone...something that I could not see or touch. I had to trust in all that I was taught and felt. In all honesty, I was scared. What if God wasn't real?

"Peace be still. Peace be still" Reverend Jones said as he began to pray.

"Lord, we come to you with hearts heavy and minds consumed with fear and doubt. Here we are, Lord standing in the need of prayer. Not my mother, not my father, but it's me oh Lord, standing in the need of prayer. Lord, we invite you to come into this hospital room Lord and be with Gertrude. Stand by her Lord. Cover her Lord. Let her feel your presence. Let her know that with Christ, all things are possible. There is no sickness that you can't heal. Nothing is impossible for you Lord. Instill in Gertrude a determined spirit. Encourage her to fight for the life that you gave her. Give her the understanding that no weapon formed against her shall prosper. She is a child of the most high and has favor."

As Reverend Jones prayed, I felt a warm sensation come over me. I will never be able to describe the presence that I felt. I was not alone and I knew that I was going to be ok.

"Reach down Lord from on high and wrap your ever loving arms of protection around Gertrude. Protect her from dangers seen and unseen. Fill this room with your presence, Lord. Shower down from above. We praise you Lord. We magnify you. We lift you up on high."

"Thank you Lord," I began to cry out loud. "Thank you Lord."

"Nothing on this Earth shall take the life of one of your children until her work here on Earth is done and you call her home. You are the Alpha and Omega, the beginning and the end. Nothing comes before you. Heal this broken vessel. Uplift this downtrodden spirit. Instill in her the will to fight for her life. She is needed, Lord. Her family needs her. Her children need her. We need her Lord. Bless her Lord. Bless her right now. We need ya...we need ya...Lord shower down your blessings. Saturate this place with your presence. Hallelujah! Hallelujah! Hallelujah Lord! We thank you Lord. We bless your Holy name. In your precious son, Jesus Christ's name we pray...amen and amen."

From that moment on, I knew that I was going to be just fine. The road was going to be long, but I was going to be just fine. Sometimes reaching your lowest point - when you are desperate for help - can *cause* you to accept the unacceptable... that death comes to us all. It is, at this moment, when you have to make a decision - *am I going to fight for my life or just give up?* You can either speak life or speak death over yourself. It's not until that pivotal moment, do you find out what you are made of. I choose life. I choose to fight for my life and be damned if cancer or anything else was going to destroy my will to live.

"Thank you Reverend Jones," I softly said, as I leaned up to embrace him. "God is good and gives us the strength to endure till the end. I've decided to fight for my life. Come hell or high water, I am going to fight."

"Now that's the Gertrude I know," Shirley said as she smiled at me.

"That's my sister." I laughed to myself, I'm back

In all of the praying and crying, no one realized that Sarah had been standing in the doorway.

"Sarah, honey how long have you been standing there? We didn't hear you come in."

She never said a word, but just looked off in the distance. Something was troubling her.

"Well saints, I must be making my rounds to the other sick and shut in. My work here is done. Gertrude...Shirley I want you to call me if you need me. I don't care what hour of the day it may be...call me."

"We will Reverend Jones. We will," Shirley said as she walked Reverend Jones towards the doorway.

"And Sarah, that goes for you too." Sarah never moved. She

never smiled or showed any signs of acknowledging what the good Reverend said. Something was most definitely wrong. Sarah never acted this way before, especially toward Reverend Jones.

"We may not understand God's reasoning, but we must always trust that His will is perfect. He makes no mistakes. We must remain strong in our faith and trust in the Lord."

"I know Reverend. I know and believe, but sometimes I just don't understand. God bless you Reverend and thank you again for praying for Gertrude."

"Anytime Shirley, but I wasn't just praying for Gertrude. I was praying for you all."

As Reverend Jones made his way to the hallway, he brushed his hand against Sarah's and looked her in the eyes. "God has not forgotten you either Sarah."

Without hesitation, Sarah pulled back from Reverend Jones and walked quickly into my room. "Good day, Shirley."

"Good day, Reverend," Shirley said with a perplexed look on her face as she returned to my side. By this time, Sarah had found a small corner of my hospital bed to sit on. I wanted to tell her to give me some space, but knew that this wasn't a good time to joke with her. I also wanted to ask Sarah what Reverend Jones meant by what he said as he left the room, but chose to let it go for now. Sarah just held onto my hand and stared into my eyes. She brushed my hair back from my forehead and smiled.

"She's strong Sarah. She will be just fine," Shirley said as she pulled the sheet over me.

"How do you know? How in the hell do you know?"

Something was definitely wrong. Now I know we all have been under a lot of stress lately, but I have never heard Sarah curse ...especially at Shirley. She may have thought it, but she never, ever said it out loud. Something was definitely wrong.

"Because God is good and all the time God is-"

"There is no God!" Sarah said lashing back at Shirley.

"Sarah, how could you say such a thing?"

"Look Shirley. Look around you. If there is a God, would He let all this happen?"

"God knows what is best."

"No! No!" interrupted Sarah. "What is best is that Gertrude be at home with her family not laying here sick and attached to machines and tubes."

"Sarah-"

"What is best is that Momma be alive to see all of her grandchildren and great grandchildren."

"Sarah...He knows-"

"He knows nothing! He knows all about our suffering and yet He continues to let me...us suffer."

"Sarah what in God's name are you talking about?"

"There's a lot about me that you don't know."

"Well then tell us Sarah," I begged. "Please just tell us."

"Stop," Sarah said as she immediately moved away from the bed.

"Sarah honey, don't leave. Please...please just stay with me. I need you." Sarah was reluctant and initially didn't respond. "Sarah did you hear me?"

"I'm sorry Gert. It's just...well, it's just-"

"It's just what?"

"Sissy, you said you were gonna beat this thing and look at you...you did," Sarah said standing in the doorway.

"God is so good," I declared to both Shirley and Sarah.

"And all the time God is-" With one sharp lunge, Sarah bent over holding her stomach. She stumbled as she reached for the nearby chair.

"Sarah!" Shirley shouted as she ran to Sarah's side.

"What's wrong? Should we call the doctor?"

"No! It'll pass...just a pain in my stomach."

"Are you sure?" Shirley asked again.

"Yes! I said it will pass in just a few seconds, just something that I probably ate." I looked at Sarah as she could barely stand to her feet. I caught the attention of Shirley and shook my head indicating that we should just leave it alone. If we pushed, Sarah would leave. We knew that she was acting strange, but we had to be very careful in questioning her and prying into her business. Her guard was always up, but something was different about her this time. We would never find out if we badgered her to death.

"How are you Gert?" Shirley asked me, quickly changing the subject.

"I'm fine. Just been thinking. Life is so precious and I finally realized that I have spent the majority of my life worrying about death, to the point that I wasn't living".

"The majority of your life? Girl, how about all of your life!" Shirley laughed to herself.

"Watch it Shirley. I'm sick but I ain't too sick to get up off this bed and beat your tail." We all began to laugh, including Sarah, at the thought of me getting out of the bed in my hospital gown, ass out, fighting Shirley.

"Gert, Sissy, you're one in a million," Shirley said as she smiled and looked at me. "What the hell are you looking at?"

"Gert, you don't have to be strong anymore. We're here. We'll be strong for you." I turned my head away from Shirley and exhaled.

"That's all I know how to be. I don't know how to let go and cry. I don't know how to trust others with what's going on inside. All I know how to do is put my family and kids first and put all that I am feeling on the back burner. I don't know how not to be strong.

"Gert...Gertrude look at me." I could barely look at Shirley. I didn't want to cry. Shirley stood up from her chair and turned my face forcing me to look at her. "Sarah come here," Shirley said, as she called for Sarah to move closer to the bed. Sarah wouldn't move. "Come here!"

I knew Sarah wouldn't move for Shirley. I stood a better chance at getting her to come closer. "Sarah, please come here." Sarah looked at me and with her head held down...she found her way back over to my bedside.

Shirley held both our hands and said, "All we have left is each other. Nothing...I mean nothing will take that away from us. Where you are weak Gertrude, Sarah and me will be strong. Sarah...whether or not you want to believe it, I love you. We love you and are here for you."

"Promise me one thing Shirley and Sarah. Promise me one thing right here and right now."

"Anything, Gert, anything," Shirley said as she sat on the corner of the bed.

"Promise me that you will do all you can so that this won't happen to you."

"What do you mean, Sissy?" Shirley asked.

"You know what I mean. I don't want this...cancer...to ruin your life like it has mine." Sarah turned slightly away from me and stared out the bedroom door.

"Sarah, look at me! You look me dead in my eyes and tell me you promise." Sarah refused to even acknowledge me. She released my hand and moved to the foot of the bed. "Sarah!"

"What Gertrude? What?"

"Don't you hear me talking to you? I need for you and Shirley to promise me that you will do everything that you can to prevent this from happening to you." Shirley glanced down at the foot of the bed and noticed Sarah was crying. "Hold on, Gertrude."

"No! I mean it! Sarah, Shirley this is not a joke. There's nothing funny about having cancer. Sure, I may act like everything is fine, but I'm not! I'm hurting and I'm in so much pain. Perhaps I could have prevented this from happening. I just didn't know how, but you both have the chance to get checked out."

"Gertrude, we will, won't we, Sarah?" Sarah never answered.

"Sarah, I don't know if you think this is a joke, but it's not. How can you stand down there not even answering me when-"

"Enough!" Sarah screamed. "Please! Enough." I didn't mean to push Sarah to the point of snapping, but I couldn't afford not to. I had to be the voice of reason and truth, whether Sarah wanted to hear it.

"I'm sorry. I know sometimes I can be too aggressive, but I mean well. I mean just look at me." I pulled back my blanket exposing all the tubes and bandages. "Just look at all this mess. You have to get checked out. I don't want you all to ever have to go through this nightmare." Something connected with Sarah. She seemed more curious than put off by all that was keeping me alive.

"I have no breast! They took my breast from me and no amount of praying, screaming, or begging is going to change the fact that a part of me is gone." Both Shirley and Sarah remained motionless. I know it was uncomfortable to accept and see, but it was my reality. Even Shirley turned her head for a brief moment.

"Look at me! Look at me! I have no breast! Do not let this happen to you."

I could see how uncomfortable this was for them, but I didn't care. I was getting through to them and that was all to it.

"Shirley, hand me those papers on the edge of the bed." Shirley found two pamphlets jutting out from the corner of my bed. As she pulled the pamphlets out from under my mattress, she read out loud, *How to Complete a Self-Breast Examination*. As soon as she handed them to me, I gave one immediately back to her and attempted to give the other one to Sarah. However, she refused to take it. "Take it!"

Sarah refused again.

"Here!" As Sarah reached for the pamphlet, I could feel my stomach becoming upset. I didn't want to have to do this in front of them, but there was nothing that I could do.

"Quick, hand me the trash can." Sarah, in one turn, grabbed the trash can on the floor next to the bed and placed it in front of my mouth.

"Gertrude what is it?" Shirley asked.

"Wait, wait a minute." Before I knew it, I threw up all over myself. I just couldn't help it.

"Oh, Gertrude," Shirley said as she jumped up from the bed holding the trash can.

"I'm sorry...I'm sorry," I repeated over and over again.

"Sissy, there's no reason to be sorry. What's wrong?"

Sarah wasn't able to stand the sight of me throwing up. She moved further away from the bed, but still kept an eye on me. She was watching so intensely.

"Do you want me to call the nurse?" Shirley asked.

"No, no I'll be fine in a minute." I knew this was too much for Sarah to handle, but again this is my reality and my truth. Before I realized it, Sarah walked back over to the bed and began to wipe my forehead with a cold cloth and started changing my clothes. "Thanks, Sissy. Thank you."

"What happened, Gert?"Sarah asked.

"Chemo" was all I could manage to get out. Sarah stared me straight in the eyes. She had this look about her...a look that pierced right into my core. "Sarah, what is it?" She never stopped staring. She just looked deeper and deeper into my eyes.

"Tell me about it." I didn't understand *what she was asking*.

"Tell you about what?" By this time Sarah had leaned into

me, still searching to find the answer to something in my eyes.

"What does it feel like?" Sarah quietly asked. "Tell me what it feels like, Gertrude."

"Stop it Sarah. You're scaring me."

Shirley didn't move; she didn't utter one word. We both were unsure as to why Sarah was acting the way she was acting. It didn't make any sense. "Tell me Gertrude. I need to know."

"Stop it!" I screamed while pushing Sarah away from me.

"Enough!" Shirley interrupted. Soon, Sarah slowly backed away from the bed and sat lifelessly in the chair in the corner of the room. "Sorry, Sissy," Sarah whispered.

"It's hard Sarah, if you're talking about the chemo, it's hard on me."

"I'm sorry Gert. It's just...well it's-"

"Don't! There's no need to apologize, Sarah. What I'm going through, I would never wish on my worst enemy."

"Oh Gert," Shirley called out as she sat back down on the corner of the bed.

"I feel weak, worn down, like the life has been ripped right out of me. The worst part is, my hair is falling out."

"It'll pass, Sissy," Shirley tried to reassure me. "It'll pass."

"I'm not sure how much more I can take of this. It's killing me."

Without warning, Sarah reached for her bag and attempted to walk out the room.

"Don't go!" I begged. "I need you. I need the both of you. I can't do this alone. Please Sarah, please, for me just stay a little while longer." She never looked back at me, but just leaned against the door and sobbed to herself.

"Honey, I can't lose my hair," I said jokingly, but was really serious.

"Ya'll know my hair is my pride and joy." Shirley began to laugh to herself. She knew that I was telling the truth. I was known for my hair. There was never a day when it was out of place. Now, I may not have had much money, but what little I did have went towards taking care of my children and keeping my hair done.

"Can you imagine me walking around here looking like a *Cabbage Patch Kid*? Y'all know that black doll saw *a rough way to go*."

Shirley fell back in the chair laughing, "Gertrude, Gertrude... only you would think that."

"Who you tellín," I laughed lying back in the bed. "Sarah, honey you know you want to laugh so just go on."

Sarah did not appear to understand the importance of laughing during a time like this. Laughter made the fear bearable. Laughter made me warm on the inside. The only thing that I had control over was my decision to either laugh *or* cry.

I was tired of crying. I was not going to feel sorry for myself. What good would it do anyway? I had no control over what was going to happen to me. What I did have control over was my decision to laugh my way through the pain.

"Sarah, you can stay hemmed-up in that corner all you want and feel sorry for me, but I am going to laugh." Sarah hesitated in her movement, but reluctantly turned somewhat back into the room. Shirley placed her hand on the edge of my bed and smiled in my direction.

"Gertrude, you are one in a million."

"She's *a mess* that's what she is," Sarah said under her breath.

"I heard what the hell you said over there."

"I knew you'd hear me, that's why *I* said it," Sarah said as she moved closer towards my bed. I reached out towards Sarah beckoning her to step closer to me. I couldn't quite figure it out, but something was absent in Sarah's eyes. Something was missing and it was bothering me.

"Honey, I wouldn't be me if I wasn't a mess. Now bring your tired ass over here and sit next to me." Sarah reached out towards my hand and eventually our fingers intertwined. Although I don't think she was expecting it, I pulled her into my arms and embraced her. Sarah wanted to pull away, but decided to just bury her head deep within my chest, quietly sobbing. Shirley found her way to sit on the edge of my bed and watched adoringly as Sarah continued weeping.

"That's alright Sissy, you just cry until you don't want to cry no more." I held Sarah tightly and laughed to myself, as I envisioned myself looking like a Cabbage Patch doll. "Could you see me walking around here looking like a Cabbage Patch Kid?"

"You'd be the finest one there is," laughed Shirley. Sarah found the strength to sit along my bed and gave herself permission to laugh, when she wanted to continue crying.

"They'd have to come up with a new name for your doll. Something like the Gertie Gert," Sarah chuckled to herself. "You couldn't be no ordinary Cabbage Patch Doll. You'd be the finest and most envied doll in the store." Shirley stood up from the bed and pretended like she was this newly created, special doll of me. "She'd have earrings on down to her shoulders; a scarf draped around her neck; and-"

"The best pair of shoes this side of town," we all chimed in together. "Don't forget a string in the back that when pulled would say you can kiss my black-"

"Gertrude" Sara said, as she covered my mouth with her hand.

Laughter soothes the soul. It made me forget all about lying in a hospital bed, fighting for my life. Our laughter somehow transported us all back to our childhood...three little black girls...sisters sitting on the front stoop... having the time of our lives.

"All fun and games aside," Shirley sighed. "We're just glad

you're o.k., Gert. You had us scared."

Sarah became serious and immediately stopped laughing. "Yeah Gertrude, you had us scared half to death."

"I had myself scared." I tightly held Shirley and Sarah's hands and said, "I didn't know if I was coming or going. The only thing that I knew, without a shadow of a doubt, was that I had to decide whether I wanted to *live or die*." I let go of their hands and placed both my hands over my chest and immediately teared-up, because where my hands rested, my breast once *was*.

"Right there on that surgery table, I told myself that *I was going to live*. I closed my eyes, took a deep breath, and turned everything over to the Lord and here I am."

I reached out to touch Shirley and Sarah's hand, but this time I only was able to grasp Shirley's. Sarah jumped up from the bed and stepped away. "I don't know if I would have been as brave as you."

"What do you mean?" I asked.

"I just don't know if I am or would have been as brave as you Gertrude. You're just so strong."

I reached out for Sarah again, but this time Sarah refused to lock eyes with me. I dropped my hand and quietly said, "Don't get me wrong. I mean, I still have a lot of stuff that I'm dealing with. It still is very hard for me to deal with this *blow* that I have been given."

I felt myself welling up inside. I didn't want to cry. I promised myself that I was not going to cry anymore, but damn it, there was a part of me that was so Goddamn tired of being strong all the time. Sometimes, I just wanted to scream and crumble.

"I have a lot of stuff that I'm dealing with!" I pulled my hand back from Shirley and covered my face. I didn't want them to see me cry.

"Gertrude, don't do this to yourself," Shirley said.

"Look at me! Just look at me!" I yelled out loud. "Look at me! A part of me is gone. They took my breast from me. They took my Goddamn breast from me and left me looking like this!"

Sarah collapsed into a nearby chair and slumped over with grief. Shirley did what she knew best - she attempted to fix the problem.

"Gertrude, Sissy you're still beautiful."

I didn't mean to snap at Shirley, but I guess all that pent up fear and anger towards God just needed to come out one way or another. Even if I didn't say it, He knew that I was thinking it anyway.

"Yeah right. You both have your breasts! You don't know what it's like to lose something that has been a part of you all your life. You don't know what it's like to smile through the pain and act like everything is fine. You have no idea what I'm going through!"

The room fell silent. I didn't mean to lash out like I did, but I needed to. "I'm sorry. I'm so sorry. I didn't mean to-"

Shirley grabbed my hand and placed it over her heart.

"I know Sissy. I know, and you're right. We don't know what you are feeling and going through." Sarah jolted up and attempted to run out the room.

"Sarah, wait!" I yelled.

Sarah stopped in mid-stride.

"Don't! I just can't! I couldn't deal with it!" Sarah screamed.

"Deal with what?" I asked.

"With it..." She repeated. "With...if I had what you have."

"Cancer? Of course you would." Sarah reached back for the chair and sat back down.

"No, Gertrude. I wouldn't. Couldn't tell people that I had-"

A perplexed look came over Shirley's face.

"People? We're family and you wouldn't even tell us?"

"People freak out. They would look at me some kind of way when they hear you have...*it*." Hearing the word *it* did something to me on the inside.

"Stop saying *it*. It is cancer. Does that mean you can't deal with me?" Sarah could sense that I was offended. The truth of the matter is, I was the only one who had cancer and had to deal with it. Sarah swung around in the chair and faced me.

"No, of course not."

"Well then stop saying it! You're stronger than you think. You would *fight* just like I am fighting. You would *live* just like I am living. You wouldn't *just* give up!"

"I..." Sarah began.

"*Ladies*, I'm afraid visiting hours are over and Gertrude needs her rest. Don't you Gert?"

"Stop treating me like some damn child. I can speak for myself!" Shirley covered my mouth by placing her hand firmly over my lips.

"Gertrude, don't talk to Dr. Cruz like that. He hasn't done anything to you." She knew me. If she took her hand off my mouth, I would have just continued cussing Dr. Cruz out. So, all I could do was shake my head *yes*.

Shirley pointed her motherly finger at me and said, "Be good, Gertrude. Be good."

I shook my head *yes* and smiled when she removed her hand. She knew at the right time, I was gonna tell her about herself for putting her dirty-ass hand over my mouth and stopping me from telling Dr. Cruz what he could do with his visiting hours.

Shirley and Sarah gathered up their belongings and both kissed me on my forehead. As Shirley and Sarah reached the bedroom door, Sarah turned and said, "Be strong, Gert. Be strong."

I looked deep within Sarah's eyes and said, "You too, Sarah. You too."

150

I watched them both walk down the hallway until they were out of my sight. Once again I

was left alone with my thoughts. I was afraid. I was really afraid.

CHAPTER NINE

The Truth Exposed

Some time had passed since my admission into the hospital and chemo treatments. I made Shirley promise me that she wouldn't tell Bradie why I had to go into the hospital. I know that was wrong, but I just don't think he'd be able to handle the added pressure of trying to focus on graduating and thinking about me.

Bradie was always a timid child. He led with his heart and in return, was used by many people. He's not like Skippy; you could drop Skippy off in the middle of nowhere and he would survive.

I worry about Bradie. He's naïve and tends to find the good in all people, even when there was no good to be found.

As I think about it, I'm beginning to think that Bradie would be fine. It is me that I fear for. My life and purpose has always been caring for my children and my family. It gave me a reason to be. Who would I be without having someone to care for? What would I do with myself and my time?

All Bradie knew was that I was in the hospital taking care of a female problem. With that being said, he asked no questions and I offered no additional information.

It killed me to have Bradie visit me in the hospital and not tell him the truth. Sometimes it felt like he could see right through me and somehow knew that I was lying to him. My own child...I was lying to my own child. What kind of a mother am I?

It was for his own good, or at least that's what I told myself. When he would come into the room to visit me, I made sure that I had the blanket pulled-up to my neck and my fingernails turned inward, so that he could not see that they had turned black from the chemo. I didn't worry about my hair, because I had a thick grain and could cover up the spots where my hair had fallen out. He never questioned what the female problem was and why I was in the hospital for so long. He just wanted to know that I was ok and would be coming home soon. Little did he know that I was wondering the same thing.

He would hug me and sometimes the pain from him squeezing me would be so excruciating that I wanted to scream. I couldn't. I couldn't let on that he was hurting me when he only wanted to love me. I thank God he was never around when I got sick from the treatments.

*　　　*　　　*　　　*

After some weeks passed, I got the clearance to be discharged from the hospital. I was so elated and beside myself. I finally could return to my regular life; or as regular as I could make it.

Things had changed for me. I wasn't the same old Gert. I had to keep the act up that everything was fine and would be fine. I couldn't let anyone know of the fears and doubts in my mind. Even though I was scared, I couldn't show it, especially for my children. I had to be strong for them. I'm a mother and that's what mother's do.

I'll never forget that sweet sound of the children talking in Momma's living room when I arrived home. They didn't know that I was listening. Bradie knew I was coming home and was so excited.

I loved watching our children grow up together. They were close - just as close as Shirley, Sarah and I. They were the spitting image of us. Their laughter and storytelling made me forget all about what was going on in my life. It normalized things for me.

"You know I never really thought about what life would be like without my mom," Brad said. "I mean, since my mother's been in the hospital, I realize that I take her being here for granted."

Georgie and Wendy both were quiet and just listened. This was a conversation that Shirley, Sarah and I had many nights, when we were their age.

"You talk as if she's dying or something." Georgie said. He was the spitting image of Shirley. Although Georgie had a heart of gold, he, like Shirley, was the most in control of his emotions of the three. *Control*...well both Shirley and Georgie understood how to keep their feelings in check. They didn't make rash, emotional decisions.

"No, that's not what I'm saying,"Bradie explained.

"I know that she's not going to die...one day will die..." Bradie became more and more frustrated having to explain himself and attempting to explain what he had always feared facing - me not being here.

"You know what I mean Georgie!" Bradie shouted. "I'm sorry...it's just a lot for me to think about at times."

"I understand exactly what you're saying Brad," Wendy chimed in. "My mother's my best friend. We do everything together." Wendy lowered her head and paused for a brief minute to gather her thoughts.

"It never really crossed my mind that she's not going to be here one day. Haven't you ever thought about what life would be without your mother, Georgie?"

Georgie took in a deep breath before answering. Sure Georgie did, but he never really talked about it out loud. The feelings that were arising found their way smack, dead in the middle of his throat, causing Georgie to swallow a couple of times before he could answer.

"Of course I have. I just don't think about it every waking moment." It sounded cold. That's not how Georgie meant it, but it was how he had to say it, so that he would not cry in front of Bradie and Wendy.

"That's just life. We are all born into this world, live and-"

"Die..." both Bradie and Wendy joined in.

"Yes, we die." Again, silence filled Momma's living room. It brought tears to my eyes to see my babies thinking about what life would be like without us. One thing helped me find some peace in all this - that they would always be there for each other, no matter what.

Soon the silence was filled with a small giggle coming from Wendy. Her smile made me smile. "You know what I used to do when I was little? I used to close my eyes and hold my breath just to see what it might feel like to be dead."

Bradie knew exactly what Wendy was talking about and found it funny himself. "God, you too? I used to turn the lights off and sit in the dark with my eyes closed too. It seems silly now, but it was serious back then." All three laughed uncontrollably.

"How the hell did we ever come up with the idea of holding our breath and sitting in the dark would ever make us feel like we were dead?" Georgie bent over in laughter.

"Do y'all remember the stories told to us when we were little? Like when Aunt Ida said that Uncle Jimmy died and saw Heaven, but it wasn't his time to go."

"Oh my God! Do I," Bradie fell back laughing. "I hated those stories. Mommy used to talk about seeing dead relatives coming back to visit her."

"Right, right," Wendy agreed.

"She would always tell me that she would see Uncle Lenny walking around the apartment scaring her half to death," Bradie continued. "That messed me all up. I mean, how am I supposed to sleep with Mommy talking about dead people walking around the house?"

Bradie was oh so right. I would tell him that I saw Lenny around our old apartment. Lenny and I talked to each other many times. It made me feel like he was watching over me.

Wendy got up and picked up a picture of Nanna and Poppa's 50th Wedding Anniversary. She smiled and held the frame close to her heart.

"You know, after Poppa died, it took me a long time before I could come back up and visit Nanna." Bradie and Georgie gathered around Wendy, holding each other as they looked at the picture.

I couldn't take it anymore. Watching them from afar made me feel like I had died and was watching over them. I wasn't dead and sure as hell didn't want to pretend like I was. Shirley, Sarah and I walked-on into the living room and joined our children. I hugged Bradie so tightly and didn't want to let go. I know this was confusing to him, as he knew that I wasn't a touchy feely kind of person, but I just couldn't help myself.

"What are you three up to?" I asked. We all found somewhere to sit and continued our conversation.

"Nothing," Bradie said as he relaxed back into my arms on the couch. "Nothing at all. Just sitting around talking about life."

Just hearing the word life warmed my heart. I so desperately wanted to live...to live life to its absolute fullest that I almost couldn't contain myself. I wanted to scream. I wanted to explode and just be freed from all the muck and mire that consumed my life for so long. All I could do was look at my baby and say, "Life, what a beautiful word."

I felt that lump form in my throat and knew that I wasn't going to be able to contain my emotions much longer. "Listen, I'm gonna go change out these clothes," I said as I excused myself.

I knew everyone...well at least, Bradie was looking at me. I don't know if I was trying to convince myself that I was buying the lie or Bradie was. Before I could even finish my thoughts, I knew the answer - I was trying to convince myself. Bradie, sure as hell, knew that there was something wrong with the way that I was acting. He knew that this wasn't the Mommy that he was used to. Who the hell do I think I'm fooling?

It's funny, denial can kill you. I mean, you rationalize, minimize and even flat-out lie to yourself long enough, *you soon will believe your own lies. It becomes your truth.* After a while, you will lose yourself in your make-believe world and will never be able to find your way out.

Soon as I made it to the top of the stairs, I heard Bradie say, "Is there something that you all are *not* telling me about my mom?" Shirley knew that Bradie was onto them.

"What are you talking about honey?" Shirley asked.

I know my son. It was only going to take so much before he started raising his voice and demanding the truth. "Am I the only one who sees this? I'm not sure how to describe it, but is there something wrong with my mom? She seems so different."

Shirley was panicking. I could hear it in her voice. "Brad, I think she's acting just fine to me,"

"Yeah Brad, can't your mother just be in a good mood and just be happy?" Georgie asked. I heard the plastic seat covering over the couch make that God awful noise whenever someone was attempting to unstick themselves. Brad must have stood up and started pacing.

"Come on, this is my mother that we're talking about. The woman always complains about everything and now she's talking about how beautiful life is."

"Brad, you're overreacting," interjected Georgie. I knew that Georgie's comment was going to send Bradie through the roof.

"I'm not overreacting! This is my mom I'm talking about and you all are just sitting there acting like nothing is wrong when something clearly is. Now, just stop it!"

"Hey," interrupted Sarah. "I have a great idea. It's been a long time...let's go out to eat as a family." I could hear everyone stirring around with excitement. We have been through so much lately.

"That is a wonderful idea," Shirley agreed. "Why don't we go to the Pike Diner? It's close and has good food."

"Stop it!" Bradie screamed, one more time. "Stop it! Somethings wrong and you all are not telling me."

My heart was breaking. How could I continue lying to my baby, knowing that he was hurting? I just couldn't bring myself to tell him the truth. Telling him would hurt him and not telling him was hurting him.

As the family continued talking, I went to my bedroom to undress. I smelled like a hospital - that smell that reminded you of sick people...death. I had to get out of these clothes.

"Brad," Shirley called out. "We will talk about this later. Trust me, your mother is fine. She's better than fine. Now why don't you go on upstairs and tell her that we are going to the Pike. You know she loves their Veal Parmesan...and so do you. Let's just have a nice dinner together."

As I unbuttoned my blouse and slowly slid it off of my left arm, I caught a glimpse of my reflection in the mirror. For the first time, I finally saw what I looked like since having my breast removed. It was almost too unbearable to take-in. My breast was gone with nothing left but an indentation in my chest where my breast once was.

"Oh, God," I cried out. "How could you do this to me?"

I was so caught up in my pain that I didn't hear Bradie calling me, as he walked up the stairs, towards my bedroom.

"Mom? Can't you-" Before I could grab my blouse to cover myself, Bradie had opened the door and saw the truth.

"Mom!" He screamed as he stared at my scared chest. "Mom! Oh my God, Mom!"

I couldn't move. I couldn't call out to him to let him know that everything was alright and was going to be alright. I just stood there with my eyes fixed on the look of fear on his face.

"Bradie! Wait, honey!" I screamed.

There was no waiting. He would never trust me from here on out. I had lied to my child to protect him and only hurt him in the long run and most definitely destroyed our trust.

"No!" He continued to shout over and over again. "No...no... no!" Bradie slammed the bedroom door and ran back down the stairs. By this time, the family had heard the commotion and became more and more alarmed by the sound of Bradie running hysterically down the stairs.

"Baby wait. I can explain."

Despite the soreness in my chest and left arm, I threw my blouse back on and ran as fast as I could after him. Shirley attempted to hold Bradie, but he was too distraught.

"Brad, hold on a minute. Just hold on one minute."

"Get off me!" He screamed as Shirley did her best to restrain him. "Don't touch me!"

As I made it to the bottom step, I was out of breath and surged with pain shooting down my arm. Both Georgie and Wendy ran up to help Shirley hold Bradie.

"Brad hold on a minute," Georgie said as he attempted to calm Bradie down.

"My mom's...my mom's," He tried to get out.

"Your mom's what?" Wendy asked.

"What happened?" He asked over and over again. "What happened to you Mommy?"

"Bradie! Bradie please let me explain."

"What happened...what happened?"

"Aunt Gert, would you please tell us what's going on?" Georgie begged.

"Ok everyone just calm down. Just calm the hell down!" Shirley shouted.

"Baby, I'm sorry. I am so sorry for not telling you the truth. I wanted to...deed God I wanted to, but just didn't know how."

"What is going on?" He cried out.

"Okay, let me explain."

"No lies! No more lies," He pleaded.

I had to tell him. No more lies. No more stories. No more deception.

"Do you remember the time when Mommy fell on her way home from work?"

Bradie knew exactly what I was talking about. He dropped his head and began to weep. "Yes."

"Well it was worse than Mommy wanted to let on."

"I knew it. I knew it."

"Yes baby, it was worse than I thought. I'm sorry, baby. I didn't mean to hurt you. The truth is...the truth..." Why was it so hard to tell him the truth?

"The truth, Bradie, is that Mommy found out that she had cancer."

"Cancer!" he screamed.

"Baby, I had cancer. Mommy didn't go into the hospital for female problems. I went into the hospital to have my breast removed and to have chemo and radiation."

"What! You lied to me?!"

Bradie then looked at both Shirley and Sarah and yelled, "You both knew and didn't tell me? You stared me in my face everyday knowing that my mom had cancer and you didn't tell me? How could you?"

Shirley attempted to pull Bradie into her, but he jerked away from her.

"No! Don't you touch me."

"Bradie, baby, don't be like that. They were only doing what I asked them to do."

"I don't care! I don't care!" he screamed with such anger in his voice. "I'll never forgive you. Never!"

Shirley turned away from Bradie and said, "I'm sorry baby. I wanted to tell you, but it wasn't my place. Forgive me...please?" I cautiously walked over to Bradie and placed his hand on the side of my face.

"Baby...I'm sorry. I didn't want to worry you since you had so much on your mind. I was wrong. Honey, don't worry. Mommy is fine. The doctors believe that they got all the cancer and that's good enough for me."

He gently collapsed into my arms weeping.

"You and your brother are the reasons why I fought so hard to live."

As I rubbed the top of his head, I kept on repeating over and over, *"Mommy's fine. Mommy's fine."*

CHAPTER TEN

An Old Friend Comes to Visit

I learned many valuable lessons about myself over the next couple of weeks. Funny, the most important lesson that I learned was that I always expected to be unhappy. I was scared to dream.

Where did this come from? If I didn't dream, then how could I expect my children to dream? I learned to live in uncertainty and permitted fear to dictate my every move in life. I wasn't living, I was merely dying a slow, painful death. I was just existing. I think I even tricked myself into thinking that I had this cancer-thing beaten, but I was sorely wrong.

Although there were no signs of cancer physically in my body, the damage that it had done to my mind was irreparable. I struggled on a daily basis wondering if and when cancer would come back and take me out this time. Cancer had taken its toll on me and I was growing tired. The thought of giving up was consistently lurking in the back of my mind. To some degree, I had to learn how to make peace with cancer and accept that it would always be a part of my life in some way, shape or form.

Despite my struggle with not becoming so deeply depressed, I always seemed to find the strength and determination to fight the blues away and vow to live my life to its fullest, or at least learn how to live life for the first time. There had to be more to life than anxiety, panic attacks and immobilizing depression. There just had to be.

I had to learn how to respect cancer even though it did not respect me. It was trying to kill me every second of every day. Do you know what happens to a person who is violently stripped of their passion and desire to live...to fight? Was it too late for me to live? I didn't even know that I had a passion to live, until it was ripped away from me. God, why did it take having cancer to find out that I want to live? I want to live... dammit, I am going to live!!!

If cancer was going to take me out of here, I wasn't going to go without a fight. I was going to go kicking and screaming. If cancer wanted a battle, I was up for it! Do you hear me cancer? I am not going to go without a fight!

What seemed like hours, was probably no more than two to three minutes. However, I didn't realize it until my alarm clock went off, snapping me out of whatever day dream I was in. My mind was racing and my breathing was erratic. It was 7:00am and time for me to get up and start my day. I only had a few minutes before Sarah would be turning the lock on the front door and calling my name out loud.

I needed to get up and eat something. Food just never tasted the same after having chemo. I don't know why, but it just didn't taste the same. It's bad to have to force yourself to eat when you just don't want to. Not only did I need to eat, I had to eat. I was losing weight by the pounds.

You better be careful what you ask for because you just might get it. I was always a thick sista and tried my hardest to take the weight off, but just couldn't. I walked everywhere and still couldn't lose the weight. If I had to do it all over again, I would have been grateful for my thickness. I would have loved every curve I had. Well, I guess that's what I get for not being specific in my prayers. I was more worried about losing the weight, than how I was going to lose it.

"Gert," Sarah called out. "Gertrude, I'm here. Come on before you make yourself late for your treatment."

Treatment...I was so damn tired of hearing that word. I wanted to scream.

"To hell with the damn treatments", I screamed out to Sarah.

Sarah never said a word. She knew that every morning, I was going to give her the shit for making me face my truth and not allowing me to paint my reality any other way than what it is.

"You finished?" she asked.

"I'm on my way down Sarah," I said, underneath my breath.

"Be there in a second." I know that God doesn't put more on you then you can bear, but dammit. I'm tired and I just didn't want to fight today. I wanted one day...just one day to be a normal day...a day just like everyone else.

I wanted to walk around the house with my housecoat on. I wanted to boil some hot water and have a cup of tea and eat a piece of toast. I wanted to watch *The Young and the Restless* and hear Shirley cuss-me- out for calling her during her story-time. I wanted to...I wanted to...

"Dammit!" I yelled.

"Gert," Sarah called out. "Gert, it's gonna be alright."

"I know, Sarah. I'm just so damn tired of this." Sarah gave me permission to wallow in my self-pity for only so long. She knew I was struggling. My pity was soon interrupted by the sound of the tea kettle whistling.

"You want sugar or no sugar?" Sarah asked.

"Sugar, please." I shook myself free from whatever moment I was having and got myself together. All I had to do was wash my face and get dressed. I took a nice hot bath last night and packed my bag.

Once I got myself together, I stood at the bedroom door and

looked back at my bed.

"God, Thank you."

I was grateful that God saw fit to allow me to get up from my bed one more time. He did his job and now I have to do mine. I made my way down the stairs, stared Sarah in the eyes and smiled.

"You are gonna get through this Sissy," Sarah said, as she gently stroked the side of my face. "We are gonna get through this together."

"I know, Sarah. I know." I said, leaving-out the front door. Sarah followed, making sure that the lights were all turned-off and the front door was locked.

Sarah was good to me. She never complained. She never said that she didn't have time to take me. Both Shirley and Sarah were there for me every step of the day. I don't know what I would do without them.

As we walked down the walkway to Sarah's car, I had no idea that today was going to be a day like no other. I was so consumed by cancer that, although I desperately hoped for good news, I didn't really expect to survive this battle.

I had no idea that today I would hear my doctor tell me that I didn't have to take the treatments anymore. Sometimes life can give you so many sour apples, that when you finally get a chance to taste the sweetness of a peach..in your mind, it still tastes the same.

We weren't at the hospital for long before Dr. Cruz informed me that I was cancer free. They couldn't detect any cancer in my body. I couldn't believe what I was hearing. No more cancer. No more treatments. All I could do was just sit there for a minute holding myself as I rocked in my seat.

I have to be honest. Yes, I was so happy to hear what I longed to hear for so long. But somewhere deep down inside, I grappled with my fear. I was afraid. I couldn't even be totally happy thinking about if the cancer was really gone or was it lying dormant somewhere and would come back with a vengeance. Sarah knew me and knew the headspace I was in.

"Don't you even dare do it. You beat this thing and that's that." Sarah got me together. "Do you hear me?" If I didn't shake loose this fear thing, it was gonna run me for the rest of my life.

"Do you hear me!" she yelled.

I turned to face Sarah, stood up straight and shook myself back to having some sense. "Yes! Yes!" I screamed over and over. "Yes!"

"That's the Gert I know."

"Dr. Cruz said no more cancer and no more treatments. You beat this thing, Sissy. You said that you would and you did it." Sarah ran over to me and hugged me like she never hugged me before.

Although we both cried tears of joy, Sarah just sobbed like a baby in my arms. "No more cancer! No more cancer! No more cancer."

All I could think about was how faithful God is. I pulled back from Sarah, as I felt myself becoming overwhelmed with happiness. My legs just seemed to crumble from underneath me. Sarah broke my fall as we just embraced each other on the floor. Dr. Cruz smiled as he walked to the door. Before leaving, he just stood in the doorway looking at Sarah and me. I whispered to him, "Thank you."

Dr. Cruz shook his head and mouthed back, "You're welcome" and gestured for me to call him later.

Sarah and I sat in our silence for a minute or two before laughing at the sight of the two of us sprawled-out on the floor crying like two big babies. I slowly got myself up off the floor and pulled my clothes together. I had not taken notice that Sarah remained on the floor. I wanted to say something to her, but it seemed like I would be intruding.

"I'm so happy for you, Gert," Sarah cried. "So happy for you."

"I know you are Sarah," I answered. Sarah didn't move. I began to walk over to her, but was stopped by Sarah holding out her hand stopping me dead in my tracks.

"Don't," Sarah quietly said to me. "Don't, I'm fine."

Something felt wrong...*really* wrong, but I couldn't put my finger on it. As a sister, I could feel it all throughout my body. I was in tune with both Sarah and Shirley, as they were with me. Something was wrong. Despite what Sarah had asked me to do, I was going to do my usual Gertrude thing and simply be blunt in my approach. "Sarah, what in-"

Before I could finish what I was about to ask, Sarah stood up, grabbed her keys and opened the door. "I'll bring the car around."

"Sarah, wait!" There would be no waiting...no explanation. I was gonna let Sarah have this time, but there would be no next time like this. Although I wanted answers, I know the feeling when you just don't want to be pushed into talking about something that you're not ready for. If pushed too hard, the backlash would be ugly.

The car ride home was tense. We both just stayed to ourselves never talking about what just took place. I didn't even realize that we hadn't even turned on the radio.

"Do you mind?" I asked before turning on the radio. Despite being sisters and loving each other, Sarah could be funny about her things and people overstepping their boundaries. Without looking at me...without saying anything, Sarah turned the radio on. I wanted to cuss her out for being so cold about it, but knew that my cussing would only be met with a good old cussing out, right back. "Thanks."

As we pulled up to the house, I could see Shirley's car parked out front. She said that she would be home by the time we got back. There are many things that you can say about Shirley and being on time is one of them. Sarah pulled behind Shirley's car and parked.

"Sorry," Sarah said softly.

"It's okay, Sissy," I replied. I found myself feeling overwhelmed. Every bit of emotion that was denied to be expressed came rushing back to me. "Oh, God. Thank You," I began to cry over and over again. "*Thank you*."

Sarah sat right with me with tears running down her face. We both were thankful. Perhaps for the same reason or maybe for different ones, but we were both thankful. As we walked up the walkway, Sarah placed her arm around my waist. "You did it Sissy...*you did it*."

As I opened the door, my normal routine kicked in. I felt like the old Gertrude again. I immediately began straightening up things around the house. Nothing was really out of place. "Gertrude," Sarah said laughing to herself. "What are you doing?"

"Straightening up," I answered.

"Girl, there's nothing to straighten up."

"Honey, you know me. It's just what I do." Never missing a beat, I kept doing my thing. I fluffed the pillows, straightened the magazines on the coffee table and cracked a window to let some fresh air in the house. Not too much cause Lord the one thing I hate the most was being cold. "Shirley...Shirley," I called out, not realizing that she wasn't in her normal seat smoking a cigarette. "Shirley? Where the hell is she?"

"I don't know," Sarah said. "Her car's outside, but where is she?" There goes those sisterly instincts again. I could feel her, but couldn't see her. "Maybe she's upstairs looking out the back window."

Both Sarah and I climbed the stairs, winded and all, making our way to the back room. Just as I thought, there was Shirley sitting in Mama's rocking chair staring out the window.

"Lord Sissy, didn't you hear me calling you?" I said out of breath, as I sat on the corner of Momma's bed. Shirley never answered. Sarah eventually made her way into the room as she laughed to herself. "It don't make any sense; being so winded after walking up just a few steps." Sarah stood at the door leaning against the wall.

"Sissy, you think we have it bad. Honey, have you ever watched your sister right here make her way up the steps," I said pointing at Shirley. I busted out laughing thinking about Shirley holding one knee and inching her way up the stairs just cussing and a fussing. Sarah and I cackled to ourselves as we thought about Shirley climbing the stairs. "Sissy, I may be older, but I sure as hell get up the stairs faster than you," I said to Shirley.

Shirley never moved, never laughed. Normally, if I said something out of my mouth like that Shirley would have every so politely put me back in my place.

"What the hell's wrong with you?" I called out, snapping my fingers at Shirley. She never moved and without any warning, one tear streaked down her face. Sarah and I looked at each other.

"Honey, what's wrong?" I asked.

"Do you know what it's like to be me?" Shirley asked. "Do you know what it's like to always be in control everyday of every minute of every second? To always have the right answer at the right time? To always know what to do, when to do it, and how to do it?"

I didn't know where all this was coming from, but I knew that it was serious. "No, Sissy, I don't."

"Do you know what that pressure is like? It's hard being me. People always assume that Shirley will know what to do, when to do it and how to do it. Shirley will fix it. Shirley's got the answer. Shirley will say the right thing, at the right time to make it all better. Shirley, Shirley, Shirley!"

"Honey-" I interrupted.

"Well, I don't! I don't have all the answers. I can't always make it better!"

"I don't understand Shirley. What's this all about?"

"I um...I ...look...look at me!" Shirley shouted. "Gertrude, I've lost control! I don't know how to fix it this time."

"Fix what?," Sarah asked.

"I can't fix this, like I couldn't fix Momma. She just laid there in the bed dying and there was nothing I could do about it. I couldn't make it go away. No matter what I did, I couldn't fix it. I couldn't change the fact that she was sick and was going to die. They looked at me for the answers. What could I have said to make it all better? What was I going to do to ease everyone's pain?"

Shirley stood up and hit the windowpane. "Nothing! Nothing! I couldn't do anything like there's nothing I can do to fix me!"

"What are you talking about?" I screamed, as I made Shirley face me.

"I took your advice and went to my doctors. I got the call today. My first mammogram, my first damn mammogram and I found out that I have cancer."

"What?!" Sarah and I both screamed.

"What are you talking about?" I asked Shirley. I couldn't believe what I was hearing. "Why didn't you tell us? We would have gone with you and supported you. How could you?"

"How could I? How could I? What the hell do you mean how could I? I'm Shirley!! I hold things together. I'm in control. If I lose it, then what? Who will fix it then? Huh? I fix things... I don't need to be fixed! I take things head on and deal with it. I make things better. I don't need any...any...I... I can't anymore. Gertrude, Sarah...I can't. I just can't."

I rarely saw this side of Shirley. She was always in control. If she needed to scream, holler, cry, she did it when we weren't around. I wanted to reach out and just hold her, but something in me wouldn't let me. We all had our roles to play and we functioned as best we could in those roles. "Shirley, we're here sweetheart. We're here," was all that I could muster up to say.

"I can't. I just can't do this anymore Gert. I can't make it right! What am I going to do?" The hell with roles and boundaries. My sister needed me and would just have to get over me holding her.

"It's gonna be alright, Sissy. It's gonna be alright," was all that I could say. This was too fresh for me. Maybe I was trying to convince myself that I was gonna be alright. The fact of the matter is, we didn't know if we were gonna be alright. All we could count on was that we had each other.

"How can you both continue asking God for help? I have prayed to God for so many things to answer so many prayers and yet..." Sarah turned her back to us and stood in silence. "...never mind." Sarah must have known that I was going to have something to say.

I took one step towards her and said, "Sarah, God-"

"Oh, no not now!" Sarah bellowed as she bent over.

"Sarah!" Shirley cried out.

"Don't you ever speak to me about God!" Sarah yelled.

I was stunned. I never heard Sarah say such a thing. "Sarah, what in God's name is wrong with you?"

"He took Momma away from me. He hurt you and now he is about to do the same thing over again with Shirley." Shirley slowly walked towards Sarah and placed her hand on her shoulder. "Sarah, Sissy, I'm not dying."

"Not yet! Not yet! It's just a matter of time." I quickly joined Shirley's side and said, "Sarah, don't talk that way."

Sarah forcefully pulled away from Shirley and became

hysterical. She began screaming and yelling. I've never seen Sarah act this way. She was the quiet one...never showing her feelings. "No...no...no! You see what I'm talking about?"

"What Sarah?" Shirley asked. "God! God! That's what I'm talking about."

"Sarah, we will be fine," I tried reassuring her.

"No we won't!" We tried to hold Sarah, but she wasn't having it. "Don't touch me! Please...please leave me alone. I'm so sorry."

"Sarah wait-" I begged her.

"Don't! I'm not ready yet." Sarah ran downstairs, slammed the front door and sped off down the street. "Something's wrong Shirley, really wrong."

"Yes, but what?" Shirley quietly returned to the rocking chair and sat staring out the window. "I sure as hell don't know, but... wait, oh God! I almost forgot about you."

"Gertrude, stop. I'm o.k. I just had to let it out. I couldn't hold it in anymore. I'll be just fine honey. Don't worry."

"What about Georgie?"

"I will tell him, only if there is something to be concerned about. Until then, there is no sense in worrying him over nothing."

"Shirley, I never meant to yell at you."

"I know Sissy. I'm gonna go on home and get me something to eat. You need to do the same thing."

Shirley and I embraced. "Congratulations."

"For what?"

"No more cancer."

"How did you know?"

"Dr. Cruz called right before you two got home to check on you and told me."

I laughed to myself. "That damn Dr. Cruz. He can't keep his big mouth shut for nothing."

"Oh, Gertrude, don't be so hard on him. He was only being nice."

"Nice, my ass. He was running his mouth." Shirley chuckled as we walked down the stairs to the front door. "If you need me-"

"I know Gert. I'll call you. Trust me, I'll be fine."

"*Promise?*"

"Promise. Again, Congratulations, Sissy."

"Yeah. Congratulations." I shut the door behind Shirley and locked it. "Some congratulations."

CHAPTER ELEVEN

Letting Go

No matter how many times you visit a hospital, you never get used to the smell of sickness. It seems to linger in every nook and crevice and is unforgettable. The smell gets trapped in your clothes, in your hair, skin, and *even* your mind. For me, it is a constant reminder of a past that I so want to forget. There are times when I'm not even in the hospital and I still can smell sickness.

I just can't forget how cancer tore my world apart, leaving me with the task of putting all the pieces back together again. It wasn't fair; it isn't fair, but that's the way life...my life was...is.

I dreaded going to see Shirley in the hospital. My mind always seemed to play tricks on me. I was healed. I was cancer free, but no matter what I told myself, I always seem to see me lying in the bed with tubes running in and out of my body keeping me alive.

The fear of death lurking and hovering over was almost too much for me. There were many nights where I wanted to just give up; nights where I begged God to take me out of my misery and to call me home, but for some reason He kept me alive. I have to admit, I was mad...mad as hell with God for keeping me in such pain. I trust Him, but that trust in Him is truly being put to a test.

I was afraid to look at Shirley lying motionless in her hospital bed. I struggled with being able to see just Shirley and not me in the bed. I know Shirley isn't going to die or at least that's my prayer, but you never know with cancer knocking at your front door. You pray and pray and tell yourself that God knows best, but-hell I might as well say it - if I'm thinking it, He already knows it. If God is so powerful and can heal the sick, then why are there so many people in the hospital dying...sick...in pain? Why?

I don't know how long I was standing in the doorway to Shirley's room, but I found myself jarred back to my senses when I heard a faint, familiar voice calling me. "Gertrude, well, are you just gonna stand there all day?"

"Oh, Lord," I said, as I laughed to myself entering the room taking a seat next to Shirley's bed. "My mind Sissy, my mind."

"Your mind, what?" Shirley asked, as she laughed at me trying to get my thoughts together.

"Forget it," I said in an attempt to avoid answering. The truth of the matter is, I didn't know what to say to Shirley. What was I going to do to make everything better for her? She is the strong one. She is the one who knows what to say, when to say it and how to say it. That's what she's good at. Me...*well*, I'm just-

"Gert," Shirley called.

"I'm alright. You don't have to worry." She knew me. She knew that I was struggling with being out of my comfort zone. I'm good at changing diapers, feeding people, caring for the bedridden, but knowing what to say...saying it in the right way...well, I always seem to mess that up or *so I'm told*. I say what I got to say and that's that. Funny, we're both strong, but in different ways.

"How ya feeling Sissy?" I asked as I fluffed her pillow trying to make it as comfortable for her as possible

"Oh...God that's so much better. Thank you Sissy." Shirley could be in pain and wouldn't tell us. I don't think it had anything to do with not wanting us to worry about her or not wanting to burden us, but it was more like just being able to deal with life on life's terms. Shirley always told us that we are born into this world...we live and then we die. Pain and suffering is inevitable. Shirley would always say that focusing on it and allowing it to rule your life was a choice. "Sore...just a little sore, but I'll deal with it."

"I know you will, Sissy," I said as I wiped her forehead. I don't know why I was wiping her forehead. There was nothing there to wipe. I guess I just wanted to touch my sister and to let her know that I was here for her.

I would catch Shirley looking at her chest from time to time. I know that look...that look of fear...sadness...that look of disbelief. A part of you is gone...gone and will never return. As I sat back in the chair, I picked up a magazine and began flipping through the pages. I wasn't interested in what I called myself reading. I wasn't even looking at the pictures. It was just my way of not dealing with the look on Shirley's face.

"The worst part for me is-" I began to say before being interrupted by Shirley, "Feeling like your breast is still there and then looking down and seeing that it's gone." Shirley pulled the sheet up close to her chin and rested her hands over her chest. She wouldn't look at me. She just stared up at the ceiling with this blank expression on her face. She stared so intensely that I found myself staring right along with her. "It's gone," she began to cry. "A part of me is gone and there's nothing that I can do about it."

I closed the magazine and just rested my hand on the side of Shirley's bed. "I often sat up in my hospital bed, and still do, wondering who would want me looking like this? Am I still attractive and desirable?" I could feel that lump coming up in my throat. I didn't want to become emotional in front of Shirley because that would only make her mad. She wasn't insensitive. She just didn't cry much. She would always say to me that crying doesn't really solve anything.

"I just didn't want to feel less than..." I continued. "...less than other women."

"I've decided not to take the treatments." Shirley's words caught me off guard. I didn't know if I was hearing her right, but it sounded like she said that she wasn't going to take the treatments. "What?!" I shouted.

"I've decided not to take the treatments."

"Shirley...why?"

"Think about it, Gert. You've been there before. Your hair fell out. Your fingernails turned black and you always felt sick. I don't want that for myself."

"I know but-"

"You've heard the same speech before Gertrude. The chemo is there to kill the cancer if it-"

"Doesn't kill you first," I interrupted.

"No chemo and no radiation, Gertrude. Now that's that."

"Shirley, you're right. I was sick all the time, but it worked. I'm cancer free."

"Yes you are, but I have to do what is best for me."

"I just don't want anything to happen to you Shirley."

"Well that's out of our hands, isn't it? The doctor believes that they caught it in time and that's enough for me. I'm not going to live life, however much time I have left, in fear. I've never allowed fear to dictate how I lived my life before and I'm sure as hell am not going to start now."

"Fine. I just don't want to lose you."

"And I don't want to die either."

"You're right. You know me. I just get caught up and let my

emotions get the best of me."

"I know, but today, well let's just enjoy the moment and worry about tomorrow when and if it comes. Now turn on my stories." As I reached for the remote to turn on the *Young and the Restless*, I realized that Sarah was standing in the doorway.

"Oh Lord. Sarah you scared the hell out of me," I said as I turned the television on.

"How long have you been standing there?" Sarah didn't say a word. She just stood there staring out into the hallway.

"Girl you hear me talking to you?" Sarah leaned her head against the panel of the door and sighed. Whatever was holding her attention in the hallway was more important than answering my question. The one thing I hate most in life is to be ignored. Shirley knew it. She knew that Sarah had about three seconds to answer my question before I came out my mouth. "I said-" as I shifted in my chair.

"Gertrude, not now," Shirley whispered to me as she gestured for me to help her sit up in the bed. "Something's not right."

"Sarah, you want to come in and have a seat?" Shirley asked. Sarah still wouldn't say a thing. Enough is enough.

"Now damn it, I've had enough," I shouted as I stood to my feet. "You've been acting crazy these last couple of months and I've-"

"I'm sorry about the other day," Sarah interrupted as she continued to stare out the door.

"It's just, well, it's just a lot." Something was different about how Sarah was talking. Yes, I know she's quiet and can be distant at times, but something just wasn't sitting well with me. I could feel my blood pressure going down, 'cause honey I was about to jump on her with all that craziness. I could see Shirley shaking her head at me telling me to calm down and to sit my crazy ass down.

"Okay, I know," I whispered to her.

"We understand," Shirley said.

"Well, I sure as hell don't." I thought I had whispered my answer to myself, but Shirley heard me and slapped the side of the bed telling me to shut up.

"Sorry."

I guess Sarah heard it too and didn't like what she heard. Before I knew it, she had spun around and looked me dead in the eyes. "It's been a lot and I don't need your smart ass comments."

Shirley knew that whether it was or wasn't a lot, I was gonna get that tail good.

"Gertrude!"

"Alright, alright, but she better watch it. Love her to death, but honey, she ain't gonna talk to me like that. We all got stuff going on and I'm barely dealing with mine."

Sarah made her way into the room and stood by the bed. I could see in her eyes that she was struggling and it was getting the best of her. I felt bad for jumping at Sarah the way that I did. I didn't mean to snap at her, but being in the hospital with Shirley and just getting out of the hospital myself was taking its toll on me.

Deep down inside, I was still afraid that the doctors didn't get all of the cancer and that it was just waiting for the most opportune time to kill me. Not only kill me, but kill Shirley too. It took Momma out of here and was doing its best to do the same thing to me.

"I'm sorry Sarah," I said as I stood up to hug her, but in true fashion, Sarah drew back from me. "I didn't mean to yell at you both."

"It's ok Sarah. I's ok," Shirley said. "We didn't either."

Sarah turned her back to us again. "It's just..."

I took a step towards Sarah and said, "Sarah, you don't have to say anymore. We really understand."

"No...no...you don't Gertrude."

"Yes we do. You have a lot on your mind-"

"Momma's gone," Shirley added. I've been sick. Shirley is-"

"No. That's not it," Sarah interrupted. "Please just let me-"

"Times are difficult, our children are all growing up."

"We're getting a little bit older,well maybe you are, Gert," laughed Shirley.

"I'm dying!" exploded Sarah.

"What!?" Both Shirley and I screamed.

"Gertrude, I'm dying. Dying!" Sarah shouted.

"What the hell are you talking about? You can't be dying!"

"I am!" Sarah fell to the ground holding her stomach rocking back and forth.

"No, you're not! You're just exhausted. Now, get up!"

Sarah wouldn't budge. I tried pulling her up, but couldn't. "Get up! Get up do you hear me?"

"No, Gertrude. Stop!" Sarah begged. I continued pulling on her. I was angry...confused...mad as hell. I didn't understand what Sarah was saying and sure as hell didn't want to accept it at all.

"Wait a minute Gertrude!" Shirley yelled attempting to get out of her bed. "Wait a minute!"

"I've got cancer and they say it's terminal!" Sarah cried.

"What are you talking about?" Shirley asked.

As Sarah wept on the floor, all I could do was quietly sit beside her and hold her. She was hurting. We all were hurting.

"Gertrude!" Sarah cried, as she continued holding her stomach. "It hurts. It hurts so much. I didn't want to tell you all." I placed my hand on her stomach and sobbed. "Oh God! No more! I can't take it anymore. Help me! Help me!" Sarah yelled. "Oh God...Shirley...Shirley what do I do?"

"Okay, okay, everyone just calm down. Just calm down," Shirley pleaded, as she tried to make some sense out of what was going on. "Now listen to me Sarah, please just tell us everything from the beginning."

As Sarah struggled with getting herself together, I helped her to her feet and sat her on the edge of the bed. I didn't want to let her know, but I was still mad. I wasn't really mad with her. I was mad with cancer. How dare you do this to me and my family? We didn't deserve this. We didn't deserve it at all.

"Sometime last year, right after Momma took sick, I went to the doctors for a routine examination. The doctor suggested that I have a mammogram since I had never had one before. So, I did and a few days went by and I received a telephone call telling me that they found a mass on my left breast and that they wanted to complete a biopsy." Shirley reached out and grabbed both Sarah and my hands.

"Okay, so it sounds like you may have caught it in time."

"I didn't follow up."

"What!?"

Sarah dropped her head and couldn't look Shirley and me in the eyes. She knew that she made a mistake and couldn't take it back. If only she could take it back. "Oh, Sarah," cried Shirley.

"I know. I know. I should have, but I was scared."

I could feel my temper getting the best of me. I wanted to lash out, but knew that it wouldn't have made one damn difference. "It's not just going to go away on its own," I explained.

"Sarah. It just gets worse," Shirley added.

"It did! *It did*! I found out when I finally went back to the doctor, that it was cancer and that it spread to my kidneys and now it is in my stomach. That's why I have the pains that I do."

"Oh, Lord!" I screamed.

"What did the doctors say?" Shirley asked.

"Nothing. There is nothing that they can do but try chemo to buy me some time."

"Well, that's what we'll do. We'll call-"

"No we won't!"

"Why not, Sarah?" Shirley asked.

"Did you hear me? It's too late. I have run out of time."

I was at a loss for words. For the first time in my life, I was at a loss for words. Was I hearing this correct? Sarah was going to die. My baby sister was going to die and all I could do was sit there and watch it happen?

"No!" I shouted as I walked away from the bed. "No...no... no God!

"I've been thinking about this for a long time now." Sarah grabbed me by the hand and pulled me back to be with Shirley. Tears were just streaming down her face. Sarah seemed to be able to gather enough strength to force a smile on her face. I don't know if this was for our benefit or hers, but she smiled and said, "You can help me die with dignity. I don't want to die alone."

"No Sarah...don't talk like that. We will get through this together. We'll find the best doctors and they will-"

"Gert," Shirley said, as she shook my hand forcefully.

"Sarah is this why you are so mad with God?"

"Yes. Why me? I tried my best to live a good life. I'm kind to others...giving. I love my family...grew up in the church. I prayed to Him daily to remove this thing inside of me and He never answered."

"Sarah, don't give up. He healed me," I said, begging her to stay in the fight.

"Exactly...He healed you, but not me. Please don't get me wrong. I'm happy for you both, but at the same time, why did he heal you and not me? I'm sorry. I don't expect you to be able to answer that. It's for me and God to work out. I just ask you to promise me one thing."

"Anything," we answered.

"When my time comes, just hold my hand. Please just hold my hand." Out of all the things that were said to me in my life, I cannot seem to get Sarah's voice out of my head. I can hear her saying over and over again, "Please just hold my hand."

Everything else from there on out was a blur. Shirley eventually was released from the hospital and her prognosis was good. She was right. She didn't need to take the treatments. She was determined to beat this monster.

I was determined to beat this...this-

IT's going to kill my baby sister.

Damn it!

CHAPTER TWELVE

The Promise

How come time seems to pass so quickly when you know that the very thing that you love most in the world will soon be taken away from you? You wish, plead, and even beg for God to grant you just a few more precious moments to sit with, talk to, and even laugh with that special person. You beat yourself up for taking the small things in life for granted. You realize that all the time and energy you put into so many of the wrong situations and people were not even worth it. You attempt to suppress your anger and sadness when you realize that the simple things in life are overlooked, minimized, and often forgotten. It's not until you are faced with the grim reality that no matter how loud you scream, no matter how many things you throw, no matter how many promises you swear never to break again, the end result is always the same: you are not in control. Death does not care about your feelings. Death does not bargain. Death is neither friend nor foe. It is just what it is, death.

My pain runs deep. My suffering has been long, however my memories are so sweet. Death may have taken their bodies, but it will never be able to take their spirit. It will never, ever be able to take my most cherished memories. For this, I am most grateful.

Some time had gone by and Sarah had withered away to next to nothing. I almost didn't recognize her. She had lost so much weight and was frail. The only thing that reminded me that this unfamiliar face staring off was my sister was the innocent look in her eyes. I just wanted to cry. As each moment passed, it seemed as if cancer was stealing my baby sister away from me bit by bit. I felt so helpless and had promised myself that no matter how bad things got, I was not going to let cancer take away the promise that I made to Sarah. If it took all my strength to walk this last mile with Sarah, I was going to. She would have done the same for me.

As we rocked back and forth on Momma's glider on the front porch, a warm breeze caught Sarah's attention. "Mmm...that feels good."

In that split second, I allowed my mind to recall the countless times Momma, Shirley, Sarah and I sat in this very same spot laughing and smiling as if we had no cares in the world. Things were different back then. We had troubles. We even had heartache, but Momma knew how to make things better. We were shielded from the problems that Momma and Daddy faced. All we had to do was just be kids; smiling, running, jumping, laughing...just kids.

"Do you remember that time after we played softball and we were riding in the back of the truck and the kids started throwing rocks at us?" I laughed as I hoped the memory would bring a bit of happiness to Sarah and ease any pain she was in.

"I had a temper back then. If they were gonna throw rocks at us, I sure as hell was gonna throw rocks back at them. They may have missed, but I made sure that I beamed one of them right in the head...throw rocks at my sisters...you better think again." I laughed and laughed thinking about how Sarah and Shirley slid down in the truck trying not to get hit. I had some balls back then-still do. I stood up and dared them to hit me if they could. If I could have jumped off that truck and gotten to one of them, I would have beaten some good old tail.

"Lord, those sure were the good old days." Sarah didn't laugh, didn't smile, didn't do anything. She sat motionless staring off into the sky. I wonder if she could see Heaven. If she could see Momma and Daddy. You know they say that when a person is about to leave this here old Earth and start transitioning, they talk about seeing people who have gone on. I've heard so many stories told by Aunt Ida and Aunt Hattie about people who saw Heaven, but it wasn't their time so they had to return back to their bodies.

I was just a talking and talking and Sarah had not made one sound. I was afraid to look over at her. "Please God just give me a few more moments with her," I said quietly to myself hoping that God would grant my prayer.

"Sarah you hear me talking to you?" She still didn't answer. "Sarah!" I called out as I shook her a little.

"Yes?" Her voice was very weak and cracked as she tried her best to answer. When I looked over at Sarah, I noticed that her lips were dry and cracked. I know when I was in the hospital; I would love to eat ice chips. They kept my mouth moist and throat from getting sore. Something as small as ice chips and Vaseline brought such pleasure to me. Ice chips and Vaseline; thank you, God for the small things in life.

"You want something to drink?" I asked, hoping to hear her voice one more time. I tried not to allow myself to keep saying that this would be the last time for everything, but each thing that we did I cherished as if it was gonna be the last that we would ever do together again.

"Please," Sarah answered.

I loved a cold Ginger Ale. When I was in the hospital, Bradie would sit by me and help me drink Ginger Ale while lying in bed. He was so kind and gentle. He would place a straw in the can and put it up close to my mouth and I would just sip and sip and then let out one old belch. We would laugh as he would say to me, "Mom, that's not lady like." I continued laughing and let out another belch and said, "How's that for lady like?" I figured with all that I had been through, I was entitled to a belch here and there."

I opened up a can of Ginger Ale for Sarah, placed a straw in the can and put it up to her mouth. Once again Sarah was staring off and did not even realize that the straw was touching her lips. "Sarah," I called out. "Take a sip."

Sarah's eyes glanced down at the straw as she slowly placed her wrinkled hand gently on my hand, trying to help me hold the soda close to her mouth. I tell you, this was hard to see.

"I love you, Sissy," I said as I wiped her mouth and sat the can down on the side of the glider.

Just as we finished sharing our moment, Shirley drove up, parked and made her way up to the porch.

"Hey, Sissy," Shirley called out to me as she pulled up a chair closer to us.

I laughed to myself or at least I thought to myself, but Shirley must have heard because she smiled and said, "Yeah honey, we all can't fit on the swing anymore."

"You got that right," I said. "These hips are unforgiving."

"Sarah?" Shirley quietly called out. "You know your hips have spread just as wide as ours." I think because Sarah didn't laugh, it caught Shirley off guard and reminded her that we had moved past the times of laughter.

"Sarah, don't you hear me talking to you?"

I looked at Shirley and said, "She's been like this all morning. I thought if we sat out here, it would jar her or something, but it hasn't."

Shirley sat back in the chair and just looked at Sarah. "She's been like this all morning?"

"Off and on," I answered. "There were some moments when she smiled and somewhat laughed, but she's just been staring out all morning."

"Has she called anyone?"

"No, not yet."

"Yes, I hear you," Sarah said out the blue.

"You scared me there for a minute. What were you thinking about?"

"I don't know, so many things." Sarah turned and looked at Shirley and for a brief moment she seemed to be herself again.

"Hey, Sissy," she said, as she smiled at Shirley. "I didn't see you there."

The look that came across Shirley's face was heartbreaking. All this time we thought that Sarah was aware that Shirley was sitting on the porch with us and she didn't even know. Shirley wiped her eyes and smiled. "I'm here, honey."

"You know what?" Sarah asked. "I think God is mad at me."

"No, no, sweetheart," I said, as I put my hand on top of hers. "No, God loves you."

"Yeah, He is."

"What makes you say that Sarah?" Shirley asked.

"Why else would He let me suffer like this?"

"Sarah, don't say that," Shirley pleaded.

"He hasn't answered any of my prayers."

I couldn't bear hearing Sarah talk like this. I wanted to fix it... fix everything and make it like it used to be. "God loves you Sarah and so do we."

"It's o.k. We stopped speaking to each other a long time ago. I guess I showed Him, huh? I'm hurting inside and it's just not fair."

"You didn't do anything wrong Sarah," reassured Shirley.

"No! I must have. Why else would He let me suffer like this?"

"Stop it! Stop it!" I yelled. "You didn't; oh Lord! Shirley what if she's right? Why her and not me?"

"Gertrude, I don't know, but if that's the case then why not me?"

"He's selfish," Sarah said as she reached for the can of soda.

"I got ya Sissy," I said as I put the straw back up to her mouth again. This was too much for Shirley. She turned her head and stared out into the street and said, "Sarah! You better watch what you say or He might-"

"Strike me down? Send me to Hell? It's too late for that."

We all fell silent. Shirley and I didn't know what to say. What could we say? Maybe Sarah was right?! Maybe God was mad at her for something she did or didn't do ?!

"Do you know what it's like to know that you are going to die? Do you know how that feels and what that does to you? No, of course not. You're cured, Gert, and you're cured, Shirley. I'm dying."

"There is no cure!" I screamed out.

"I live in fear on a daily basis thinking this is going to be the day that it comes back and kills me. I'm so afraid of dying that I can't even enjoy living."

"They caught yours in time. Mine is still living and breathing inside of me and it's killing me. It's killing me!"

"Sarah..."

"No! No! No! There's so much that I don't have. Please don't take my feelings away from me. Let me have something. Please let me have something." Sarah fell silent again and just stared off. "I would give anything to turn back time. I'd change so much."

"Like what?" Shirley asked.

"I would have screamed when I first found out. Do you know that I just sat there and didn't say anything? I just sat there... silent. I guess, I figured, if I didn't *say* that I had cancer then it wouldn't be true. I would have cried instead of shutting down. Crying helps you know? So much pressure inside me. There's so much pain. I would have fought for my life instead of just giving up." Shirley reached across the glider and grabbed my hand.

"I would have talked to someone. I've been silent for so long. I want to live, Gertrude. Shirley, I wanna live."

"You *are* living Sarah," I said. "You are *alive*."

"This is not living. Look at me. I'm sick. I am really, really sick Gertrude and no amount of laughter or joking around will change that. I'm going to die."

"Don't you talk like that!" Shirley shouted out.

"I'm going to die! I'm sorry. It's just not fair. It's...just not fair." Suddenly, Sarah winched over in pain and fell to the ground. "Oh God!"

Both Shirley and I quickly moved to Sarah's side. Sarah began rocking back and forth...breathing heavily... screaming in pain.

"Sarah! Oh God Shirley, what should we do?" I screamed.

"Let's get her back in the house," Shirley directed.

"No...no please I want to stay out here." I rubbed Sarah's stomach and just cried.

"Sarah you need to get some rest."

"No...no....there will be plenty of time to rest. I'm sorry. I just have to be honest with myself." 'Dammit," I yelled. "How could you!"

"Gertrude, calm down," Sarah laughed to herself. "I'm the one that's dying and should be mad. Not you."

"Wait a minute Sarah. Don't think for once that you are the only one who has ever been mad with God or even questioned God. You're not the only one who felt like God didn't answer their prayers. I had many sleepless nights crying and begging Him to save me."

"That's right. Do you think that I just Thanked God when I found out that I had cancer?" Shirley added. "Sometimes I doubt God and question why He lets certain things happen. I wasn't fine when I was told that I had cancer. I was mad...mad as hell, but what could I do about it? Really, what sense did it make for me to complain and to be angry? It wouldn't change the fact that I had cancer or have cancer."

"No, I have cancer," Sarah shouted.

"No, *we* have cancer! The only difference is you know yours is there. I don't know where mine is. *Remission!* What the hell does that really mean anyway? I live in fear on a daily basis. I am so scared Sarah!" Shirley yelled.

"Me too, Sarah", I added. "It doesn't have to be cancer. It could be anything that kills me, but whatever time I do have left, I don't want to spend it being angry. I'm not going to beg or ask for mercy. I will not spend any more time wishing that I had said what I wanted to say but never did. I'm tired of feeling trapped and allowing fear to control me."

"I'm sorry," Sarah said, as she held both our hands.

"Sorry for what?" Shirley asked.

"Gertrude, Shirley, I wanted to reach out to you both all my life, but..."

"Sarah, you don't owe us any explanation," I told her.

"No, I need to say it. For me. I need you both to know that life was never easy for me. I've always sat in the background watching from a distance wanting to share, to give, to laugh, to feel or to just do more. I want you to know that I was reaching out on the inside, but couldn't on the outside. It was too much. I could only scream and hope that someone would hear me, but they didn't. Do you know what it's like to not be heard, but to be able to hear everything said about you? I hurt. I feel."

"Oh Sarah-"

"Please, I'm not saying this to change anything or for you to feel sorry for me or even to make you feel bad. I am doing this for me. Finally, for once in my life, I am doing something for me. I want to be heard. No more waiting. No more waiting."

"Oh Sarah, we know honey," Shirley said.

"It's funny, as different as we may seem on the outside, we are *so* alike on the inside. We are joined together by our pain, sadness, and our fears." Shirley was right. Regardless of which journey we took in life, our end is still the same. Death is waiting for us all.

"Our anger and hurt."

"Our joy, laughter and so much more," Sarah smiled and sighed.

"What happened to the little girls inside us who loved to jump rope?"

"To braid hair and play dress up?" I added as a tear streamed down my cheek.

"They grew up," Shirley answered.

Sarah shifted in the glider, in an attempt to stand to her feet. I tried to help her, but Sarah refused my help as she pushed my hand back. "No Gert. I got it."

When Sarah finally made it to her feet, she stumbled a little bit, but caught herself and said, "It's a blessing to be able to stand...to stand on your own."

As Sarah gathered herself, she wiped the tears from her eyes and quietly asked, "Do you remember the promise?" I didn't want to think about *the promise*. The promise we made as little girls, so long ago. How could three little girls be so young and immature, but be so in tune with life and understand the importance of sisterhood?

Shirley stood to her feet and said, "To speak only out of kindness. To love unconditionally." Sarah beamed with happiness as she looked back at Shirley.

"To take care of our parents and each other no matter what

may come our way," Shirley continued.

This was too much for me. I didn't want to talk about the promise. I wanted everything to be as it was. I wanted my sister to be alright and not die.

Sarah continued reciting the promise. "We promised to always be there for each other. To never leave angry."

Shirley grabbed Sarah's hand. "To hold each other's hand when it was time to say goodbye. We promised that the first and last face to be seen before we took our last breath would be each other's. We promised."

"We promised," Sarah said.

I couldn't say it. I refused to say it. Saying it was confirmation. This wasn't supposed to be something that we had to do. We were children making a silly promise to each other that was never supposed to come true. It was pretend. We were just children having fun...passing the time along. This was not supposed to be-

"Gertrude, Sissy," Sarah called out for me. I heard her and knew what she was attempting to do. She wanted me to promise. I didn't want to promise. I wanted things to get better.

"Gertrude!" Shirley said sternly. She could yell all she wanted. I was not going to make any Goddamn promise.

"Oh, God!" Sarah screamed as she fell over.

"Sarah! No! Please God no," I pleaded as I attempted to stop Sarah from falling to the ground.

"Shirley, help me."

"Say it! Say it!" Sarah screamed over and over.

"Please Gertrude, Say it! Say it!" Sarah without warning bellied over and fell to the ground. "Sarah, sweetheart, get up. Get up Sarah! It's Shirley."

"Help! Somebody! Help!" I called out. Shirley and I pulled with all our might and finally somehow managed to lift Sarah to her feet and sat her back on the glider. "Say it Gertrude!

Please, just say it!"

"Sarah, I Promise!"

I promised her as I wrapped my arms around her and just held her and continued to say over and over, "I Promise! I Promise! I Promise!"

"Sarah, we're here. We promised honey. We're here," Shirley said. "We're here."

Sarah was able to get herself together as she rested back in my arms. I began to swing the glider back and forth. It seemed to soothe her...me too.

"There you go," Shirley said to Sarah. "Just try to calm yourself and relax."

Sarah turned and looked at me. She smiled and even laughed a little. "How come everytime I see you, you're crying?" Both Shirley and I couldn't help from laughing.

"Hell, you know me. It's what I do best."

"Gertrude, Shirley, I'm afraid I don't have much time left. I wish I could take back all the time wasted on trivial things... things that just don't matter. Things that got in the way of me telling you Gertrude and you Shirley how much I love you, and how grateful I am to call you my sisters. I need you to promise me that you will take care of my Wendy. Tell her that I will always be near, watching over her."

I looked at Shirley. We both knew that our time left with our baby sister was drawing near. "We will," Shirley and I cried.

"I need you both to help me with one last thing. I've said some ugly things to God. I was scared and angry. I thought He forgot about me. I need you to help me talk to God."

"Help you?" I repeated.

"Please."

"We will. Where do you want to begin?" Shirley asked, as she took in a deep breath.

"You see, that's just it. I haven't talked to God in such a long time. I've cursed Him, blamed Him, and even turned my back on Him. I thought He hated me...that he forgot all about me. I even thought that I did something to deserve this, but *I was wrong*. God doesn't want us to suffer, but sometimes through our suffering comes understanding. Cancer has taught me to cherish every second of every day...to value the gift of life."

Sarah grew silent. "Oh God...the pain...the pain is gone. He wants me to be with Him. I can hear Him calling my name. Oh God... you did hear my prayers. I'm so sorry...thank you. It's beautiful...so beautiful."

With one last gasp, Sarah closed her eyes and called out, *"Momma!"*

"Sarah? Sarah! Sarah, No! Please, Sissy come back!" I begged. "Sarah!"

"Oh, Lord. She's gone, Gert." Shirley wrapped her arms around the both of us and gently swung the glide back and forth.

"She's gone, Honey. She's with Momma and Daddy. Watch over us, Sissy."

The End